Table of Contents

> ## Front and Back Cover Illustrations
> ## by Laura Givens

Spring Fever

I'm juggling several different projects as I assemble this spring issue of *Tales of the Talisman*. I just approved and refined edits of the new edition of my wild west steampunk adventure *Owl Dance*, coming soon from Sky Warrior Publishing. I also have just finished working through a new draft of its sequel, *Lightning Wolves,* and turned that into the editor. Now, I'm writing a horror novel set at an observatory not unlike those I've worked at called *The Astronomer's Crypt*. The hope is that novel will be out for this Halloween.

All of these tasks require that I sit inside at the computer working away. That's easy on those windy, dusty blustery days we get in New Mexico sometimes, but a bit more difficult on those nice days when the temperatures are mild and the sun shines in a blue sky. Not helping matters this year, my daughter is heading off to college. One of her choices is in New Orleans. We decided it would be worthwhile if I traveled with her.

One of the things I like doing best on a clear, spring day is to sit outside—or in the passenger seat of a car on a road trip—and wile away the time with a good book. It's not been at all difficult for me to make time to slip off and reread these stories prior to publication. You'll find some fine escapes for a pleasant spring afternoon including Jennifer Crow's "The Root of the Matter" in which two people, who find themselves homeless through circumstance, must battle a dragon, or Ian Brazee-Cannon's tale of aliens spending "A Night at the Club."

We'll also be sure to give you something to think about after you finish these stories. Jeff Samson takes a look at what it would have been like to have been a soldier stashed away in the Trojan horse. Dan Bracewell will make us think about the notion of swimming with corporate sharks in his story "Pool Sharks."

I hope these and the rest of the stories and poems contained herein will tempt you away from work to a nice sunny place to enjoy a tale well told.

—David Lee Summers

Tales of the
Talisman

Volume 9   Issue 4

ISBN: 1-885093-74-8

William Grother
Publisher

David Lee Summers
Editor

Laura Givens
Art Director

Kumie Wise
Assistant Editor

Tales of the Talisman
(ISSN 1558-0377)
is published quarterly by
Hadrosaur Productions
P.O. Box 2194
Mesilla Park, NM 88047-2194
www.hadrosaur.com

Subscriptions: $24.00 per year
$48.00 per two years
Subscriptions available at:
www.talesofthetalisman.com

Tales of the Talisman assumes no responsibility for unsolicited manuscripts, photographs or artwork. Unsolicited material must be accompanied by a self-addressed stamped envelope to ensure its return.

The Root of the Matter

Story by Jennifer Crow
Illustration by Kathy Ferrell

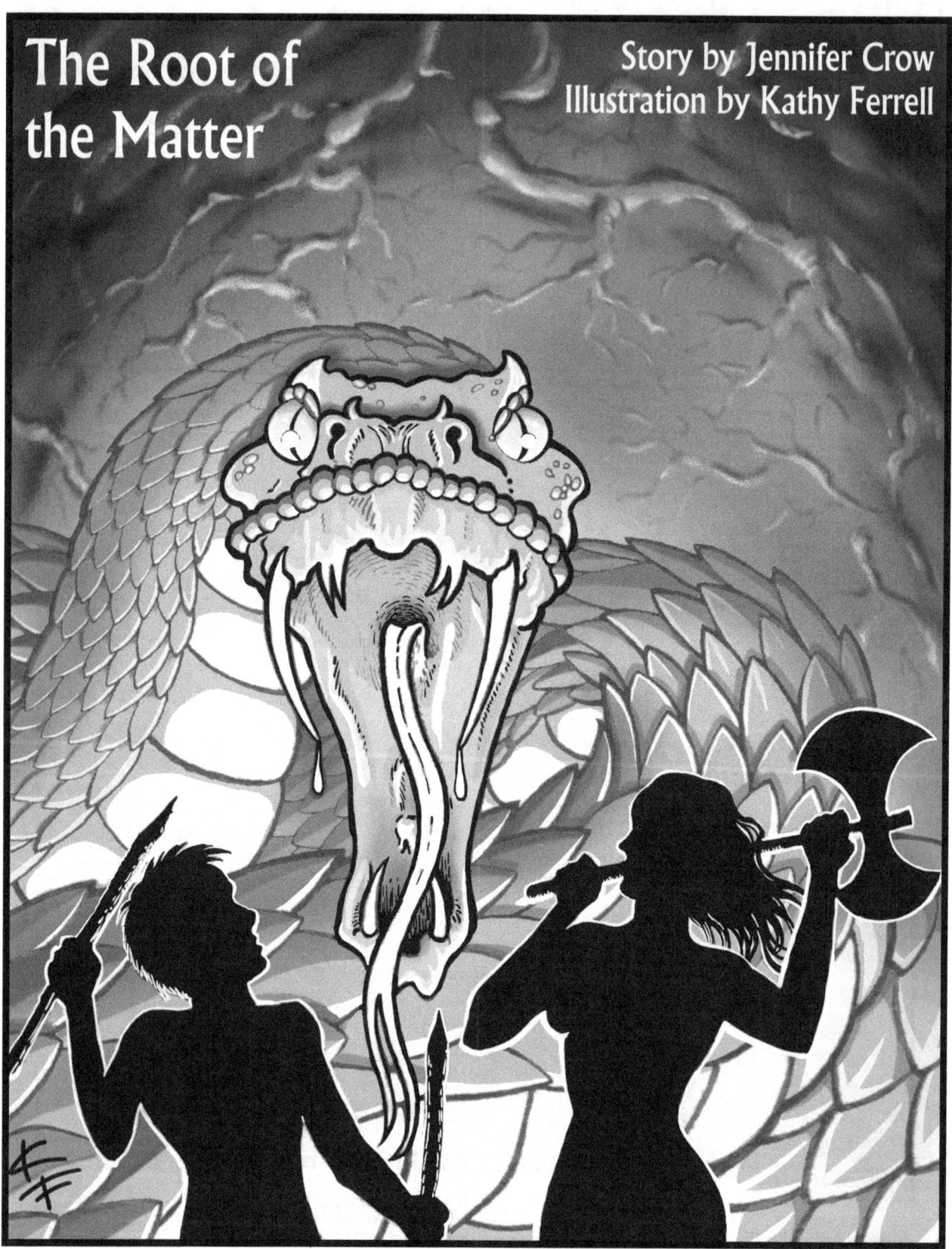

The boy, a few years younger than Maura, crouched between two roots of the big tree, his scabby arms wrapped around his knees. He had a face like a slammed door—not just closed, but violent in its rejection of any intrusion. As she had for the past three days, Maura left a plate of food at his feet and took the empty dish away.

She wasn't sure if he ate. She hadn't money for more than peanut butter sandwiches and bruised apples from the local orchard. For that matter, the red squirrel that shrieked in the lower branches might be stealing the boy's food. Maura shrugged. It wasn't her business if he chose to go hungry. She hadn't invited him into her sanctuary.

The building squatted at the edge of town. Once a hotel built on the pattern of an open square with a garden in the central courtyard, it had fallen into decay and long since been abandoned. Of the garden, only the tree remained, its thick gnarled roots rising like arthritic limbs from the dry ground. Otherwise, only a few sticks and brown leaves remained, mingled with old plastic bags and the shredded remains of fast-food meals.

The courtyard door clanged shut behind her. In her first days hiding in the hotel, she'd jumped at every sound. But it seemed the world had forgotten this place, and now she moved about as though she owned it. Most of the rooms stood empty, wallpaper peeling around the pale shadows that marked places on the wall where pictures once hung. The kitchen sinks belched rusty water and mice nested in the cupboards. In the dining room, black and white tile marked out a giant chessboard, and tired nymphs with graying limbs held up the mantel over the fireplace.

Maura had taken a room on the third floor. The roof overhead was mostly sound, only one dark stain seeping from the outer corner, and the windows had glass in them. She'd torn up the rotten carpet, and kept the floor swept. One corner held what passed for her bed, and she hung her few extra clothes from a hook on the ceiling to keep the mice from nesting in them.

She'd just chosen a secondhand book from a shelf made from cement blocks and warped boards when the door below banged shut again. Sure she'd latched it, she clutched the novel to her chest and stared at the door. She could wait here, throw the lock, she thought. But she recalled the few trespassers who'd intruded on her refuge, the ones looking for a place to hide from the authorities, or a place to smoke or shoot up or otherwise send themselves to oblivion. One stoner had almost burned the place down around her, until she'd driven him off with an old wrench and some inventive threats.

I have to see, she told herself. With the wrench in hand and a tremor in her step, she made her way past the empty mouth of the elevator shaft and opened the door of the stairwell. Slow steps echoed up to her.

Biting back the urge to call out, she leaned over the railing and saw a small, scabbed hand clutching the rail. It was the boy, climbing to her aerie.

"Well," she said when he rounded the last landing and faced her. She still held the wrench, at her side but clearly visible to him. "What brings you here?"

He shrugged and jerked his chin at her in the way adolescent males do.

"I haven't got anything else to eat, if that's what you're after. Shopping day's tomorrow. That's when the day-old bread shop has its specials."

"I'm fine," he said. "Thanks for the sandwiches."

"I wasn't looking for company."

He lifted his chin again. "I'd go, if I had anywhere else."

She stared at his arms. "They hurt you pretty bad."

He picked at one of the scabs, his gaze evading hers. "It's all right."

Silence stretched between them. She noticed he held something in his hands, a clear Mason jar with the lid screwed on tight and something colorful within. "So what do you want?"

He held out the jar, and it made a chinking sound. It held bits of glass of many colors. Mostly brown or green or clear, the color of beer bottles and mayonnaise jars and lemon juice bottles. But there were flecks of blue as well, some as deep as the evening sky and others the pale aqua of Caribbean shallows. "It's all I've got to pay you."

She tried to wave away the jar, but he pressed it into her free hand. "It's okay. I'll find more."

His dark eyes held a glint of something desperate. Shame, she realized, and recalled the burn of embarrassment she'd felt before she'd found this place. "Wait here."

Maura didn't want him to see which room she called her own, still leery of letting anyone else in. She'd been saving a few clean jars to recycle on her next trip into town, and she took the one she thought was nicest and carried it back to the boy. "For your next collection," she told him.

He surprised her, first with a crooked smile, and

then by unscrewing the lid and putting his ear to the jar's mouth. Maura was reminded of a child listening to a shell at the seashore. She was about to comment on that when the boy's smile faltered, and his gaze flickered to hers and then down to the floor.

"Are you okay?" she asked.

He screwed the lid back on with quick fingers. "It's good," he said. "Great, really." After a pause, he added, "Have you thought about sleeping somewhere else? I mean, not on the top floor?"

"I like it here." She kept her voice low and flat, not sure what he meant. She'd been afraid, since he appeared in the dusty garden, that it signaled the end of her peaceful time at the old hotel.

"Me, too," he said. "But there's something eating the tree. When it falls…"

Maura bit back a laugh. "Did your jar tell you that?"

He hunched his shoulders up around his ears. "Sorry. Thanks again for the sandwiches." And just like that, he was gone.

* * *

Maura moved her mattress closer to the window, to catch the little bit of starlight that filtered through the windows. As patterns drifted across the ceiling, she fell asleep and dreamed of shadowed halls. Red-hued eyes watched her, and she walked beside a wall only to notice the scaled pattern of its surface, and the slow movement as it breathed. Someone sang in the distance, haunting fragments that clung to her thoughts when she awakened.

She was humming to herself as she spread peanut butter on the last slices of bread. The boy—she still didn't know his name, she realized—appeared at her elbow. "You've heard it, too," he said.

"I dreamed it."

"The music? And the old hall?" He hummed the tune, the rumble surprisingly deep in his narrow chest.

"What's it called?"

He shook his head. "Dunno. It means something, though." He took the sandwiches she offered and went back to the courtyard. She followed with her own breakfast, and almost stumbled into a hole in the ground.

"What the—"

"Sorry. I heard water last night and opened it."

With peanut butter and white bread stuck to the roof of her mouth, she bent closer and saw that it was not a hole so much as a wooden hatch, now open, leading to a brick-lined tube barely wider than

her shoulders. Below, the hushing sound of moving water came to her.

"I didn't think the town had sewers," she said, once she'd swallowed the last of the sandwich.

"It's a spring," he said. "It sounds clean."

She smiled. "You hear things I don't."

"You'd hear it, too, if you let yourself listen."

"Okay." She knelt, tipping her head so she could catch any nuance in the water, but all she heard was the squirrel shrilling in the tree. The boy held out a piece of bread liberally coated with peanut butter, and the squirrel snatched it up.

"That's Roska," he said, pointing to the squirrel. "He's pretty rude, but the tree likes him. He keeps the worst of the birds away."

Roska bobbed on his hind legs, gobbling up the treat, and then darted back to the top of the tree, where he shrieked at some unseen intruder.

"He hears the thing eating the roots, too."

"So," Maura said, "he's Roska, but who are you? You never told me your name."

"I don't know yours, either," he pointed out.

"Fine. I'm Maura. I ran away from home when I was about your age, and I've been running ever since. I'm too old for them to make me go back, I guess, but I got in the habit of it."

"You know how it is, then." The boy picked at a scab on his wrist. "I'm Rags. I mean, that's what my friends used to call me."

"Rags." She extended her hand, and gave his a quick shake. Contact made her nervous, and from the look that skittered across his face, he felt the same. They parted ways as soon as their meager meal was finished. Maura washed in the kitchen's rusty water, and changed into clean clothes for her walk to town.

She returned a few hours later, carrying the usual bread and peanut butter along with some canned food from the food bank and a bag of bruised fruit she'd dug out of the dumpster behind the grocery. "Rags!" she called, "I could use some help putting this stuff away!"

He didn't answer. Annoyance shifted to a pang that surprised her. Had he left so soon? She shook off that thought, reminding herself that she didn't mind being alone. Preferred it, even.

Rags hadn't moved on, though. He was sitting in his usual spot, with his back to the tree and his legs pulled tight to his chest. He gave her a wild-eyed look and held a dirt-grimed finger to his lips.

She dropped the bags and hurried to his side. "Is there someone in there?"

He shushed her and pulled her down beside him. "It will hear you."

The flesh along her spine crept at the terror in his voice. "What will? Roska?"

"*It* will. The thing in the roots." He pointed at the hole. "It came to drink from the spring. I heard it." His eyes were red; she saw he was blinking back tears. "I shouldn't have opened it."

"It's okay. It's too big to come up that way." She thought of the wall of flesh in her dreams, the scales as big as saucers, the red unblinking eyes, and found that her reassurances didn't work as well as she might like. Rags clearly wasn't comforted, either.

"We woke it up." For the first time, his voice held a reedy, childlike note that matched his appearance. "It'll kill the tree, and it'll be our fault."

She didn't want to hug him; that seemed like too much contact for either of them. But she squeezed his shoulder. "We'll fight it, if we have to. It's our tree. Our home."

He swiped away the tears with the heel of his hand, leaving dark streaks under his eyes. "Okay." After a moment's thought, he added, "Should we ask someone for help?"

"Who would listen?" she asked bitterly. "Who would believe us?"

Rags' only answer was a solemn nod.

Because Rags worried that the serpent would attack—and because she wasn't used to anyone worrying about her--the two of them moved her mattress down to the ground floor. Rags wanted her to sleep outside, by the tree, but she told him that would be too much sky overhead. Too much company, as well, but she didn't say that aloud.

She dreamed of scales and teeth, and saw the roots of the tree with great gouges dug into them. The tooth marks looked like the fluting of columns, and where light filtered in, scales glittered like jewels. She heard a name in her dream, Nidda, and knew it was the creature whispering. It breathed out threats like splinters.

Restless in the dark hours, she rose to find a bite to eat. Rags awaited her in the kitchen, the door to the hotel's basement thrown open. A dank, musky odor rose from it that she didn't recall from her earlier explorations.

"It's the creature," Rags said when she wrinkled her nose and lit a rusty old flashlight, pointing it down into the darkness.

"Nidda," she answered absently.

"You do hear it," he said, his tone almost accusatory.

"Only since you mentioned it," she countered. The two of them finished their meal in determined silence.

"We have to fight it," Rags said at last. She didn't answer right away, focusing her attention on sealing up the peanut butter jar and the bread and putting them in the broken refrigerator where the mice couldn't reach them.

"How?"

He shrugged, with a glance that deferred the decision to her.

"All I've got is a wrench."

"More than I've got."

After a longer stretch of silence, she said, "What can we do? What do you hear?"

"We'd have to go down there to find out." He pointed to the basement, which all at once seemed more like a gate to hell.

* * *

When they entered the basement, Maura decided the two of them were like a very small, very poor military expedition. They wore makeshift packs made of folded sheets, and along with Maura's wrench they'd found a couple lengths of broom handle in the janitor's closet. Maura had done her best to sharpen those into stakes with a dull pocket knife, without much success. "Maybe it's big but skittish," she said hopefully.

Rags gave her a pitying look. Like her, he must remember the creature's watchful eyes, the slow thunder of its breath in the darkness. He heaved a shuddering sigh, and then slung the homemade spear onto his shoulder. "Well, come *on*."

The flashlight had a tendency to dim suddenly, flaring back to full brightness when Maura tapped it against her palm. The basement itself, laid out in two L shapes divided by doors, was as deserted as the rest of the building and showed no sign of Nidda.

"Maybe it was just a dream," Maura said. She couldn't keep the relief out of her voice.

"It's not in the basement." Rags crouched down along one of the inner walls. The courtyard, and the tree, would be out there, above them. He scrabbled at the cement, and Maura came closer with the light. A thin crack ran crookedly up the face of the wall, bits of concrete spalling away. "There's a breeze."

Maura laid her hand over the crack and felt it, chill and damp. It carried a smell like rotting fish. "Fine," she said. "But how do we get in there? It's not like we have a sledgehammer."

"Push." Rags leaned his thin shoulder into the

wall. Maura joined him, though she doubted it would do much good until she heard the grinding noise, and felt it shift beneath her.

The two of them kept shoving, and gradually the wall gave way. "I hope it's not load-bearing," Maura said. The whole thing slid backward as she spoke, and her words ended on a shriek as she fell into the darkness on her hands and knees. The flashlight spun around just out of reach, and then fell with a splash into water deeper than she was tall. It lighted up the stones the formed the bottom of the pool, and then shorted out with a bluish spark.

"Now what?" The darkness seemed to swallow her words.

"There's light ahead," Rags said. He found a place to stand and offered his hand. Maura clambered to her feet and brushed at the knees of her jeans, which were thick and clammy with mud. She saw what Rags meant, the faint flicker that showed where the wall curved away on the far side of the pool. To Maura's relief, a narrow walkway edged the dark waters of the pool; she eased along its length with the boy at her side. The tunnel wall was made of carved stone, not cement. And though it was in better condition, she had the sense that it was much older than the hotel basement.

"I dreamed this," Rags whispered.

"All I saw was the … creature." To call it a dragon seemed too absurd, even in this ancient passage.

"I dreamed it. I dreamed I was hunting it with my mother." His voice trailed into silence.

"You never talk about your parents," she said. They'd stopped on the far side of the ledge, and she stooped with her hands on her thighs. Her whole body trembled at the thought of going further.

"Mom is dead." He said it with the flat tone that came with both pain and practice. "I don't know where Dad is. He promised to come for me, but he never kept his promises. So I ran."

"I don't blame you," Maura said. "It can be tough." She wanted to say that if she'd been lucky enough to get a kid like him, she wouldn't have left. The words stuck in her throat, though, and after a silent moment, she continued toward the light.

The corridor opened onto a vaulted room of brick and metal. "It's a forge," Rags said. He pointed out a black anvil almost as long as he was tall. Maura had never seen one in real life before, only cartoon versions getting dropped on cartoon heads.

"Look!" Rags grabbed her arm and pointed. On the wall were hung weapons and armor—nothing fancy, but sturdy and wicked-looking.

"Perfect." She seized an axe by the handle, and found she could lift it down. The heavy head gleamed, its dark surface shading to silver where the edge had been honed sharp.

Rags, laughing for the first time she'd heard, had hefted a coat of chain mail into his arms and was struggling to pull it over his head. "It's heavy," he mumbled.

She helped him into it, and he returned the favor when she found a larger version. It bound a bit under the arms, clearly not designed for a woman to wear, but the weight on her shoulders comforted her. Rags chose a spear from the arsenal. Examining its point, which glittered like water in the light, he said, "Who do you think made them?"

Maura shrugged. "Isn't it enough that they're here?"

"I feel like we should pay."

"Yes, you should." The shadows heaved and shivered, releasing an ugly little man as thick and gray as a bar of iron. He looked over Maura and Rags and shook his head. "Thought you'd help yourselves?"

Maura tried to swallow, her mouth suddenly dry. "We're here to fight the dragon."

"Nidda?" His laughter scraped like a blade on a whetstone. "Really? What would you do that for?"

"She's killing the tree," Rags said. "It's in pain."

"Is it, now?" The dwarf scratched at his beard with a broken, blackened nail. "The corpse-sucker thinks she'll have her day at last, and you think you'll stop her? What a pack of fools." He shook his head.

"But can we borrow these?" Maura gestured at the mail and weapons.

"You can buy them." His teeth glittered in a thin-lipped smile, and he fingered a spear that had appeared in his hands.

"We don't have anything. But dragons have hoards, right? We could share with you."

"So you want me to give up my hard work—and I'm the finest smith in these halls—on the hope of payment later?" He laughed again, a sound that grated on Maura's nerves.

As she opened her mouth to hurl a challenge, Rags stepped in front of her. "I'll pay," he said. "I know you don't want gold."

"You're quicker than the woman. You may survive after all." The dwarf raised his spear and dragged the point down the boy's cheek.

As the point drew back, Maura pushed him aside. "No, not him." And then all words died on her tongue as the point burned its way into her eye. There was a popping, sucking sensation. She thought he meant to kill her, but he drew back.

She hunched down, hands over her face, and blood trickled hot between her fingers. The pain scraped her skull raw, and she keened. Rags crouched beside her. "You have to help her," he begged the dwarf, his voice rough with horror.

"Warriors take care of their own," he said. Maura looked up, her good eye blurry with tears, and saw him polishing the stained spear.

Rags ripped the sleeve off his shirt and wadded it into a ball; she pressed it against her eye and felt it give like a squashed grape. The sensation made her shudder.

Something thudded against the wall above her head. The dwarf had stepped just close enough to lean the spear over her. He gave a slight bow when she glared at him. "It's for you to name it," he said.

"Once it's earned a name," Maura ground out through the pain.

"Surprise after surprise," the dwarf muttered. "Wisdom in weak vessels. Yes, Nidda might have a surprise or two in store for her." A piece of white silk landed on the floor between them. "Use that as a bandage. You can't be bleeding all over the place down here. *She* will smell it."

Maura felt herself fading, the forge's heat washing over her in dark flames. "I need … I need…"

Rags bandaged her head, looping the cloth over her bad eye and tying the ends of the silk in a careful knot. "That's the only thing I remember from Boy Scouts."

She tried to laugh, and a spike of agony dug all the way to the back of her skull. "What, no dragon slaying merit badge?"

"If they had that, I might have stayed." Hearing the wistful note in his voice, she caught him in a rough embrace.

"Thank you. I'm glad you're here."

After patting her back, chain mail jingling, Rags wriggled free. "Hey, he's gone!"

Her one good eye took longer to focus, but Maura saw he was right. The dwarf, his fee taken, had vanished. The bandage was already growing sticky, and she had to stop every few steps to take a deep breath and lean against the wall.

"You're hurt real bad, aren't you?" Rags peered up at her with anxious eyes. "Maybe we should go back?"

"We need to stop Nidda, don't we?" She pushed herself away from the warm stone and wavered on her feet before regaining her balance. "What if she kills the tree before I heal?"

Rags looked doubtful. Maura closed her good eye and listened to the air moving through the tunnels. *Blood calls blood*, she thought. Dream memory surfaced, and she took a step. "This way."

The boy followed without arguing.

* * *

At the very least, Maura admitted, the spear made a good walking stick, and gave her a way to mind her footing. The pain in her eye had faded to a dull ache, though she suspected that was because of weariness.

"I'm hungry," Rags said, for what seemed the hundredth time.

She started to say, *It hasn't been that long*, but it seemed harsh given how patiently he'd walked. Without breaking stride, she swung the pack off her back and passed it to the boy.

There was a sound of scuffling behind her, and then he said, "There's only one sandwich left."

"Go ahead and eat it."

"But you haven't had anything—"

"It's all right. I'm not hungry." And she wasn't. She felt light—full of light—and sharp as the leaf-shaped blade of the spear. It winked at her with each step, as it caught the faint glimmers in the tunnel and magnified them.

With a grunt of pain she bent closer, and saw that the light was reflecting from palm-sized plates scattered along the corridor. When she picked one up between thumb and finger, she felt its slick surface, the whorled pattern. "Scales." She held one out to Rags, and he took it in the hand that wasn't holding a sandwich. "They're huge."

He made an agreeable sound around a mouthful of peanut butter and stale bread. "Maybe we need a plan," he said stickily.

"I don't have a good plan for dealing with a giant snake." She squinted her good eye and tried to guess how far they'd come, and how far they had to go.

Rags took the scale she held and pressed it to his ear. He made a face, concentrating, and then he let it drop. "She's close. Just ahead. I think there's a weak spot at her throat. Now what?"

"I don't know." Maura turned the spear in her hands. "I've always run before."

Something chittered ahead of them; they both crouched, weapons at the ready, and then Rags said, "It's Roska. What are you doing down here, you stupid squirrel?"

The squirrel scrambled along a root that twined along the ceiling of the tunnel, its tufted ears lifted. It stopped just long enough to snatch a bit of sandwich from Rags' outstretched hand, and vanished with a whisk of its tail.

"We must be really close," Rags whispered. "Roska's never far from the tree."

At that moment, a foul wind gusted into their faces, and a sound like glass scraping stone shrilled around them. "It's coming," Maura whispered. She set the spear before her, point out, and gritted her teeth. Nidda glittered and hissed, a blinding rush of movement that bore down inexorably.

The first blow sent Maura to her knees. She heard Rags cry out, and a clatter of metal that suggested he'd fallen. Before she could call his name, the spear twisted out of her grip, dragging behind the monstrous bulk of the serpent. Nidda was as thick as Maura was tall, and the scaly wall of her body seemed to continue forever.

Maura forced her way in the serpent's wake, her hands reaching for the spear, for Rags, for anything that might help. Her fingers caught a loose rock, about as big as her head, and she hefted it. Something was carved in it, but she couldn't tell what by touch, and there wasn't enough light to see.

The press of the serpent's body kept her close to the wall, so she didn't see the open place until she'd stumbled into it. Nidda whipped her head back, eyes of black and gold glistening as she crawled closer. The spear, Maura saw, was stuck between two scales. Of Rags, there was no sign.

"Are you looking for your spawn?" the creature hissed. "I'll suck the meat from his bones, and the fluids from his flesh. He'll need a little time to season, though. A little time to become sharp of flavor." The forked tongue flickered out, trembling like laughter.

"Give him back." The pain in Maura's head burned, and she clasped a hand to her bandaged head. It felt as though flames might come searing out at any moment, consuming all before her. But the air around her stayed cool, the serpent watchful.

"I cannot give back what I've taken. I am the ruler of this place, and what is mine, is mine." Nidda coiled up, raising her head. The spear popped free and skittered across the stone floor of the room. Maura darted toward it and heard the glassy screech of Nidda's scales. The stench of death made her gag, but she threw herself on the floor, her hands scrabbling for the spear.

The haft brushed her fingers and slid away. She cried out from frustration and fear as Nidda's thick coils bore down on her. The weight ground her into the stones, her cheek and chin burning where they scraped. As she tried to struggle free, reaching for the wall, she heard the boy call her name.

"Rags!"

"Help," he croaked. When she stumbled to her feet, she could see around the serpent, enough to see the creature open its mouth wide, unhinging its jaw so it could swallow the boy whole.

"No!" She snatched up the spear and lunged forward. The spear tip skidded off Nidda's scales with a shower of sparks, but it was enough to distract the creature. It whipped around, hissing, and tried to circle Maura. She lashed out with first the point, and then the butt of the spear, seeking for any leverage at all, but Nidda seemed impervious.

"Here," Rags called, his voice low and hoarse as though he'd been nearly strangled. "I see a spot."

Keeping her eye fixed on the serpent, Maura tightened her grip on the spear.

"Now move," she said, "so I can get a clear strike."

"Do it now," Rags told her. "Where she's weak. I'll keep her occupied."

"Rags—" She maneuvered toward Nidda's head, but couldn't find a way to reach the creature's throat without hurting the boy. So she threw the spear to him. "Do it now!" she shouted. "It's the only way!"

Rags hesitated, but saw the serpent's wide-stretched jaws bending toward him. When he struck, the spear scraped along Maura's ribs. Despite the searing pain, she took hold of the spear and leaned with all her weight as it plunged deep into the monster's neck.

Nidda screamed and thrashed, knocking Maura and Rags aside as the death throes consumed her. Even when the creature at last lay still, the two survivors didn't move. "You're not going to die, are you?" Rags asked.

Maura struggled to free her shirt where it had been caught on the spear. Her blood left a long stain on its haft. Where it and the serpent's blood smeared the wood, dark runes appeared. Though she couldn't say how, she suspected she knew what they meant. "Wyrm-Slayer." She laid a pale, trembling hand on it. With the other, she reached for the boy. "We did it, Rags."

He began to cry, harsh but silent sobs that shook his thin frame.

"Don't mourn the living." It was the dwarf. "I see you managed to name the snake-sticker."

"It's a good spear," Maura said. "Thanks."

"You paid for it." He produced a pouch of herbs and sprinkled them into her wounds, first the shallow cut on her ribs, then peeling aside the bandage to treat her eye. Before she could cry out, he had another silk bandage out, and wrapped it around her torso. "No poison. That's good."

"She'll live? You're sure she'll live?"

"Yes. Thank the gods your aim was good." When he'd finished wrapping another bandage around her head, he tucked in the ends and pressed the rest of the herbs into Rags' hands. "You'll know what to do with these now."

She nodded, a hand pressed to her temple. "It's like my brain is full of another person's knowledge."

"That'll sort itself out," the dwarf promised. "Give it a bit of time. Even Old One-Eye himself had a bit of trouble swallowing what he asked for."

"I didn't ask for this."

"No." The dwarf laid his hand on the boy's shoulder and said, "Sometimes the gods bless us beyond what we deserve. There'll always be a price, you know. You'll have to guard the well, now that Nidda's dead."

"That's not so bad." She struggled to sit up all the way, despite Rags' frown. "Rags and I, we'll take good care of it."

"Me, too?" Rags looked, for a moment, as if he might run.

"If you'd like to stay," Maura added hastily. "You don't have to."

"You want me to stay?" His thin face creased into a smile, even though traces of tears still streaked the grime. "Like, for good?"

"For good," she said. And with his help and the dwarf's rough assistance, she used the spear to hobble past Nidda's empty bulk.

Quercus Californica

dryad, of California fair
the relentless sun glares down
baking fine age lines in your bark

as a sapling you grew breathing
air thickened by particulates
the smog brown to the sight, noxious

to the tongues of your leaves
your roots delving through years
of drought and pesticides

to the snow-fed sediment beneath
a faded yellow ribbon waves
flaccid greetings to each passing car

your trunk tattooed in black letters
poorly masked in brown
"XIV"—you're property of the gang

despite your lack of Norteño red
the graffiti upon your belly
confronts the stuttering sidewalk

young men spit at your roots
you drink it in

— Beth Cato

Said Cassandra

Story by Jeff Samson
Illustration by Erika McGinnis

"Our ships!"

Chiron turns to those of us behind him. His wide eyes, set deep within his long, gaunt face, dart from man to man, searching for an explanation. He finds none.

"They're burning our ships!"

We march along the shore. At our right, men work over bonfires, roasting our ships over the twisting flames like sides of meat on spits. They swing their axes and hammers at the weakened hulls, breaking them down and bundling their pieces with lengths of rope.

At our left a row of high, jagged rocks rises like a wave frozen in time, obscuring our view of the vast stony beach beyond—where the workers are lumbering with their loads of broken boat.

Chiron's eyes lock with mine.

"Do they mean to strand us here?"

His words linger in the stinging, sooty air, hovering about us, refusing to be ignored.

To his right I see Xanthus turn toward him—the heavy brow and strong chin of his unmistakable profile rendered black in the firelight.

"Do not be foolish," he says. "They could break apart a hundred boats and there would be plenty left to take us home."

I become aware of a strange drumming—a medley of dull tones and erratic rhythms. At first it appears to be emanating from within the rock. But I quickly realize I am merely hearing echoes—that the clamor's origin is somewhere in the distance, beyond the wall.

"But ... why burn them at all?" asks Chiron.

It is not until our company rounds the point where the sun-bleached stone achieves its apex and dives sharply to meet the pebbly sand that Chiron is answered.

* * *

"Linos…"

Dareios takes my arm in his huge, calloused hand. His voice barely rises above a whisper.

"What is that?"

I do not try to respond. I do not turn to look at his face, for I fear I will find the same dread that is drawing my features taut. I merely pry his fingers loose and take his hand in mine. I squeeze hard against his grip and hope the pain will wake us both.

"My friend," he says, breathless. "Tell me what that is."

Through the haze of smoke and vapor leeching from its charred wooden hide, I make out its neck,

thick and strong, rising into the midnight sky, its mane bristling with broken rudders and oars—a stark shadow against the star-flecked blue-black. I see the hard lines of its massive head sloping down from its thirty-foot summit, the arc running from ears to snout matching that of a ship's hull. The flanks are hinged to the great cylinder of its torso, held outspread by rough-hewn struts. Rows of knotted ropes hang like viscera from its open belly, swaying between its column-sized fore and hindquarters in the sea breeze.

"It's hollow," says Chiron. His voice quavers. "They can't mean for us to climb inside that thing … can they?"

Xanthus whips his head around.

"Of course not," he says. "What good could we do inside it?"

Scurrying like rats beneath the beast, men nail fragments of ships in scale-like fashion over the last bits of naked, skeletal frame. For an instant it seems those nearest the monstrosity are much taller than the others. The men carrying boards from the fires heft their bundles above their heads to reach those completing the legs. Through the shifting bodies I see that the thing stands atop a platform—an enormous platform resting on four pairs of massive—

"Wheels!" says Xanthus, his voice brightening. "See, it's got wheels. It's a ram of some sorts, meant to be pushed. If we were inside, who would do the pushing? The Trojans?"

Some of the soldiers chuckle at the thought, but not me. The growing fire in my gut tells me Xanthus is more right than he knows. And the fury in my friend Dareios' grip tells me that he knows it, too.

I look to our left and right at the soldiers keeping pace with our formation, eyes peering at us from the shadows of their helmets—their swords drawn and shields high.

Immediately my skin goes cold. I am awash in sweat—my body pushing out moisture as if trying to rid itself of poison. My heart races, knocking against my ribs like a caged animal. My blood throbbing in my ears, I realize they flank us not as our fellow soldiers, but as our captors.

Yet still I march, obedient to my training, my legs moving against my will, compelled by some unseen force toward the monstrous steed.

* * *

A commander I do not recognize calls us to a halt at the platform. The beast looms above us, smoldering as if newly forged in the fires of Hades—a thing ripped from the scorched fabric of nightmare and sewn recklessly into the waking world.

The commander walks before us, chest forward, eyes narrowed, sizing us up, first one, then the other. When he reaches the end of our line, he whips around, feet first, then body, then head. He faces us. He smiles wryly.

"Fifty of our most fearless," he says, disbelief coloring his booming voice. "A fine gift you'll make."

His men, still stationed around us, laugh in harsh, cutting tones.

I glance down our line to see my comrades turning to one another, brows furrowed, mouths downturned and taut. A few of the men meet my gaze. It is clear they do not understand.

I want to cry out—to tell my friends to resist. To seize our captors' weapons and cut them down. To run. But I cannot. It is as though my throat has clenched shut by a ghostly hand—my body sealed in place by its own sweat.

I turn back to the commander.

A nearby fire, flaring as it is fed a pile of fresh wood, illuminates his features. Much of his face is streaked with silvery scar tissue and flecked with freshly scabbed wounds. What's left of his eyebrows clings to his skin in beads of molten hair. His mouth is a crag—the flesh below his nose and above his chin lipless and ragged. All jest has left his face.

Still holding us in his unblinking gaze, he motions to the beast.

"Climb in," he orders, "while we still have the cover of night."

* * *

We ascend, graceless. The crude ladders raised to either side of the belly are still logged with water and encrusted in tiny creatures and sea scum. Many of us lose our grip and slide down. Our captors howl with laughter as they watch us struggle.

From above, I hear the commander's men shouting.

"Tighten it up, soldiers!"

"That's right—toes to heels, beards to backs."

"Plenty of room for you all."

Dareios and I are the last to reach the belly and are thankful when Galenos, kind giant that he is, extends his titan-sized hands and pulls us the rest of the way.

Our comrades have lined up in two even rows. Dareios takes his place in front of me, leaving Galenos and me the lucky two at the rear. The nature of the beast affords us slightly more room and a fat beam where we can rest our backsides. The only such respite for the men before us lies in the crotch to their rear.

We are packed into this festering belly as if we were its entrails. We can't move, any of us. We are resigned to a slight squat, to constant tension on our thighs and calves. I've no doubt that when the beast's flanks are lowered and locked in place, there will be more flesh than air inside.

From a few rows before me, Chiron turns to face us.

"What is the meaning of this?" he says through his teeth. "Are we to be locked up and left for the Trojans to find? Where is the sense in that?"

Xanthus turns to him, his brow scrunched over his eyes, lips pursed.

"A fine gift we'll make," he says, recalling the commander's words.

"Is that what we are? Some false offering to lure them in?" says Chiron.

Xanthus shakes his head.

"Odysseus has lost his mind," he grunts.

"Are we nothing more than a trick? Than bait?" says Chiron.

Xanthus looks to me, his face reddening.

"How in the name of all the gods can he call himself our war counselor?" he hisses. "What nerve!"

"Nerve?" says Chiron. "This is beyond nerve. This is lunacy!"

I share their disbelief. If this ruse shows the extent of his craftiness, it is a wonder that our army has survived this war this long.

"They said this was an honor," says Dareios softly to himself, his head bowed.

An honor indeed. A chance to show our valor, to achieve a status beyond our meager ranks. To take part in a mission so grave that it would only be revealed to us when it began. The reins to turn the tide of ten blood-drenched years—placed in our hands. And it seems this honor hinges on a trick—a piece of guile unworthy of us.

Had I only known. Had any of us known.

Our success rests on wild assumption—on the gullibility of an enemy that has time and again proven shrewder than us. We may succeed in our ruse and deliver this poisoned gift. But we are the fools inside it.

It appears that a power once divine now rests in the hands of a man. Odysseus. Our counselor. And yet would it not be more fitting to call him our architect? For he is indeed the architect of all our fates—his cunning driving the bloodlust of Agamemnon and his piggish lout of a brother, Menelaus.

That fool, Menelaus. Would that his cock was half as short as his temper and half as hard as the back of his hand. Then he might have kept Helen at bay. And I would be home, my hips pressed firmly into my wife's backside, instead of my friend's.

These men are so bent on victory that had they enough black ships to spare, they would have sealed our entire host in an even greater vessel. Fifty. Five hundred. Five thousand. Our numbers do not matter. We ourselves are unimportant. Only our deed will secure a place in the songs of poets. Our names will be lost in the bowels of oblivion, replaced by those of greater men who watch us from afar, stomachs full of wine and lungs of sweet sea air. I am certain they already count themselves among our company.

"Soldiers!" shouts one of the men at the belly's edge. When he is sure we heed him, he motions to the front of our cabin.

There the commander sits facing us, quite comfortably it seems, in a space much larger than any of the rest of us have. Eyes narrowed to slits, he surveys our ranks.

"Warriors," he intones, "I have but two orders for you. Do not move. Do not speak." He pauses, his eyes shifting between our two rows. "I will have more when the time comes. Until then, the price for doing anything else … is your head."

He nods to his men, who sheathe their swords and descend the ladders. When they reach the ground, he orders the two of us nearest him to break from their places and pull up the ropes.

I hear more orders from below, and notice when another pair of ropes—tied many times around the thick struts holding the flanks open—are pulled taut.

Knowing what he must be feeling, I bring a hand to Dareios' sweat-slicked shoulder, squeezing tight in a futile effort to reassure him. I hear him faintly whispering, again and again.

"Madness…"

There is a breath of silence. A guttural cry from the soldiers below. A tortured creak as the beams momentarily bow before being wrenched free. A rush of cool air as the flanks fall and enfold us.

Then darkness.

* * *

We feel them before we hear them. The beast begins to vibrate with their approach. The cabin's dried-out walls squeak like a flock of infuriated birds. The synchronized thud of men marching in formation nears us, though not as quickly as we would have expected.

The pace is far too hesitant. On any other day we would take their trepidation for weakness. But today every tentative step means suspicion. A greater chance of our parting gift being investigated and our ruse revealed.

Their pace slows further. We prepare to be discovered. Our minds go to our wives and homes. Our hands to our hilts.

An ear-splitting grunt brings their entire host to halt.

Tension seizing me, I disobey my orders and shift right, bringing my face to rest against the cabin's wall. Through a gap between two boards, I peer at the world outside.

The commander dismounts his horse, followed by his two captains. He stands a full head higher than the taller of the two. Atop his broad shoulders, his silver helmet gleams bright as the sun—its shimmering auburn crest shoots toward the sky. As he steps towards us, he folds a pair of arms that look as if they were cut from stone across his barrel chest, and tips his head back. Through the helm's opening, gilded in hammered gold, I see a dark and deeply lined face that seems too old for its body.

He stops just before he slips from my line of sight. He scrutinizes the structure, his gaze shifting between the platform's wheels, moving up the hindquarters, tracing the bulging lines of the belly to where they slope to form the neck, finally coming to rest where I know the head hangs.

The captain who had been at his right—richly tanned and sinewy, tidy black curls rimming his sunken, ice-blue eyes—is the first to speak.

"Must have burned and broke fifty of their ships to build this, sir," he says.

"Fifty? I'd say at least a hundred," says the second captain, his face pale as the sand at his feet except where it was marred by freckles and sprouting fiery orange hair.

The commander raises a hand to his chin, gently pulling a tuft of wild, coiling hair.

"At least a hundred indeed, Thymoetes," he says, pausing a moment. "Seems like the Greeks had a busy night."

The captains laugh.

"Left in a hurry, too," says the dark one, stepping forward to the commander's right once more.

"Quite so," says the commander. "But why waste their time fashioning this then?"

For a moment, neither offers an answer. Then Thymoetes steps to his left.

"If I may, sir," he says, squinting up at the beast. "Perhaps it is an offering of sorts."

His counterpart laughs.

"Just hear me out, Capys," he says, grimacing at the dark captain. He turns to his commander. "Sir, it has been ten years now and in all that time there's not been one day's reprieve from battle—"

"All the more reason to suspect something is amiss," Capys interrupts. "To suddenly find our shores free of our enemy—their camps broken down, their fires put out—"

"Maybe they finally had enough."

"Enough? Agamemnon doesn't know the meaning of the word."

"Perhaps we've taught him."

"You give him too much credit," Capys grunts. "And what of this?" He motions to our hiding place. "I assume this means they've had enough as well?"

"The Greeks know our reverence for horses," says Thymoetes. "Perhaps this is how they've chosen to concede their defeat—to acknowledge our might."

Capys shakes his head, grumbling as he appears to consider the idea.

"So this ... hideous thing," he says, "is a sign of respect?"

"Oh, it's crude and cumbersome, but ... yes." Thymoetes pauses and looks to his commander. "It could be a sign of ... peace."

As the captain mentions the word, the commander's face seems to brighten.

"Peace," the commander says, as if uttering the name of a long-forgotten love. He levels his head, still tugging on his beard, his eyes wide and distant.

"Sir," says Capys, "Let us not be too hasty. We must remember who it is we are—"

"You have word from your scouts, do you not, Capys?" interrupts the commander.

Capys slowly draws a breath.

"I do, sir."

"And their report?"

"They report neither Greeks nor the boats that bore them on any stretch of shore in sight."

The commander nods for a moment, then tips his head back to consider our offering. Suddenly, he whips around to face his men.

"Trojans," he booms. "Our enemies have fled our shores—and left us a gift."

The men respond with a deafening hurrah.

"It will make a grand centerpiece at our victory celebration—and we have much to celebrate!"

Their cheers entwine, mesh, become a wall of noise. They hammer the sand and stone beneath them with the butts of their spears.

Inside we take silent delight in our victory—in their mistake that the day belongs to them. Some of us look to the man at our side and grin, others place a reassuring hand on the back of the man before them, as do I to Dareios.

Then a lone cry of dissent shatters the celebratory chaos.

* * *

A hush sweeps over the men.

I look to see where all the enemy's heads have turned. They watch as a rustling cuts towards us through a phalanx of soldiers in hurried, uneven steps—a shock of stark white hair jostling the perfect rows of gleaming helmets and spear tips, shifting like an animal through high grass.

He emerges from the sea of Trojan warriors caked in sweat and breathing hard. He lumbers toward the commander, nearly crumbling to the ground. The captains catch him by his outstretched arms and help him to his feet.

The man is old, but intent—his voice forceful.

"Sir," he says to the commander. "You must listen to me."

The commander steps to him.

"But of course, Laocoon," he says. "What have you to say?"

Laocoon. The name seems to echo throughout our cabin with a gravity all its own. It is a name we know well, one of fabled proportions, belonging to a seer of incomparable prescience. A name that, given our circumstances, instills new fear in us all.

The seer pulls his arms free and thrusts them toward our cabin.

"Sir, this is not what it seems," he says. "This is no gift."

The commander cocks his head.

Laocoon steps towards him, eyes wide and solemn.

"It is a ruse," he hisses. "Open it and you will find it carries not respect, not tribute, not peace ... but Greeks."

He knows.

"Greeks," says the commander, evenly.

"They are inside," says the old man, raising his voice. "Hidden within these blackened planks, poised to emerge when we are most vulnerable."

His ravings stir the crowd. Mumblings of Greek trickery spread among the troops.

"You are sure of this?" the commander asks.

"I saw it—clear as day—in a dream," says Laoc-oon. "In a vision sent from the gods."

The commander shifts his gaze from the seer's eyes to look up at our gift, again slowly scanning its hide. For a moment it seems his gaze locks on my peering eyes. I feel my body go stiff as a corpse's.

"Sir, you must heed me when I say there are Greeks inside," the seer cries. "They will seal the fates of us all."

Without warning and with surprising speed, the seer whirls and wrenches Capys' spear from his hand. He draws it back and aims the tip at the horse's belly. Instinctively, I withdraw my face from the crack.

From below comes a sharp grunt of animal exertion. A solid thunk shakes the planks beneath our feet. A leaf tip of burnished bronze thrusts through the wood. It projects a mere finger's width into our chamber, but hums with barely suppressed rage as the unseen shaft quivers beneath—resonating hollow, as if we truly were but dreams and vapors.

I look back through the planks to find the two captains again propping up the old man.

"We must burn it," he hisses. "Burn it!"

The words reverberate within the cavity—within the core of each man. To roast confined and helpless and very much alive is a death too honorless to bear throughout eternity.

We ready for our escape. For our end. The cabin's stillness is punctuated by the faint noises we make. Knuckles crack as grips tighten on hilts. More than one blade rings free of its scabbard's throat. If we are to die today, it will be by the sword, not the torch.

But it is only Capys who draws his sword.

"Commander!" he shouts.

In one fluid motion his sword slips from its scabbard, whistles through the air, and strikes the rocks at the commander's feet. I wince at the sharp clang of the bronze blade meeting the stone.

Amazingly the commander does not even flinch. He merely looks on as Capys slowly squats before him, and follows the captain's hand as it extends past his chiseled legs.

A sigh sweeps across the front-most lines of soldiers as Capys eases his hand from a gap in the now bloodied rocks, withdrawing from it the fat, shimmering black body of a serpent. Blood oozes over his knuckles from the cut that took its head.

The body, thick as a man's calf at its widest stretch, is so long that Capys takes several steps back before the tip of the tail is revealed. As he does, Thymoet-es—keeping firm hold of Laocoon—reaches down and retrieves its head. He brings it to his face, then squeezes at the hinges of its mouth to open its jaws. Even from my distance, I can see the slow curve of long, translucent fangs glinting like sap in the strong sunlight.

He turns to his commander.

"An ill omen on this good day," Thymoetes says. He whips his head to face the seer. "Your spear rouses evil, old man. Your words…" He thrusts the severed head to within a breath of Laocoon's face. "Poison."

"Poison indeed," says Capys. "A bite from this slithering beast would have ended any of us quite quickly … and painfully at that."

The seer's gaze shifts among the three men. After a moment, he settles on the commander.

"Sir, I assure you my words had no part in this," he says. "I beg of you—do not let this lure you from the truth."

"The truth?" shouts Thymoetes. "Since when does the truth keep such insidious company?"

"Sir—"

The commander hushes the seer with a wave of his hand. He takes the serpent's head from his captain. He appears to study it, gazing into its glassy eyes.

"This might have been my end … seer," he says, hissing the last word as if it were as vile as the snake in his hand.

He throws the head aside and steps toward the old man. He crouches down until their eyes are level.

"They offer peace," he says, pausing on every word. "And you would set their token aflame. By scorning their gift, freely given, you would risk replenishing their thirst for blood."

Laocoon's face slackens. He raises his hands and interlocks his fingers under his chin. His voice is small and falters.

"Sir, I beg of you—"

"Take him hence," the commander barks.

Two men break from the ranks and fall upon the old man.

"There are Greeks inside!" he screams, writhing in their grasp. "I tell you there are Greeks inside!"

The soldiers struggle and subdue him. His protestations fade into the distance.

As Capys and Thymoetes give their orders, we sheathe our weapons and allow the blood to return to our whitened knuckles. Their men scramble beneath us and take their places.

Capys grunts.

And the beast rolls forward.

* * *

The gates open, unleashing the roar of the crowd within. Their cheers smash into our hull like a great wave guided by the hand of Poseidon himself. The unimaginable volume intensifies the rattling of the cabin as it is pushed along the stone entranceway. Dozens of horns scream in triumph. A thunderous cavalry charge of drums rattles my heart within my chest, stirs my bowels, loosens the sinew from my bones.

A break in the shafts of sunlight pierces our cabin and moves from bow to stern. The gates shut behind us with a resounding boom.

The festival continues long into the night. The city echoes with merriment, music, the crackle and roar of bonfires. Feet stomp the marble courtyard in dance. The sunlight turns from gold to deep red and dies. Pale blue beams of moonlight illuminate us from above and quivering blades of amber torchlight from below, bathing the cabin in a play of cool and warm hues.

For a moment I enjoy the display of light. I forget the heat, the hunger, the smell, the scorching pain in my thighs. I forget the arrogance and insanity that placed me here. I consider the moon. The fire. The celestial and material glory residing outside these walls. I am reminded of the love the gods must have for us, to bless our trivial lives with such splendor.

* * *

Dareios coughs. At first I think he is only shifting his weight to lessen a burn or a cramp. But his movement is too abrupt.

The next shudder comes only moments later, this one accompanied by a muffled grunt.

It is a cough I know well—one of a stubbornness all its own. A cough that robbed us both of countless nights' sleep as children. That years later earned Dareios his share of lashings from captains who found it undisciplined and unfit for their ranks.

He coughs again.

The time between is shorter, the shudder greater, the grunt louder. I begin to see the worried faces of my fellow soldiers staring back in my direction.

They have reason for concern. The festivities have long since ceased and the city is as quiet as the dead. In the still sea air even the smallest sound rings out like a bell. If Dareios coughs when the soldiers making their nightly rounds on the city's walls and walkways are near, he will betray us all.

I bring my hand to his familiar shoulder. Wordless, I will him to stop.

Again.

The planks beneath him creak. His body tenses against mine as he attempts to squelch his spasm. But his exertion only makes matters worse.

I cover his mouth. Press hard against his lips and chin.

Again.

He places his hand over mine, doubling the pressure.

Again.

Across the darkness I find the eyes of my commander, his ruined face lit by a silver shaft of moonlight from above.

He cannot see me. My face is entirely cloaked in black. And yet his eyes, dark and blazing, tell me he knows he has my attention.

Again.

He nods.

At first I go cold. Then numb. And suddenly it is as though I am a third person, watching myself from outside my body. I wish that it were so. That I might reach out and stay my hand—stop me from doing what I know I must.

My head reeling, my heart threatening to burst within my chest—I obey.

My blade enters at the base of my friend's skull. I drive it through his brain and stop when I feel the tip bite into his brow.

He does not shudder. He does not cry out. Our bodies, tightly packed, prevent his from dropping. Our tunics, laid on the floor of the cavity, absorb his blood.

His body moves like honey, slipping gently to the floor.

Before my tears can fill my eyes, the man now in front of me steps back, filling the much-coveted space. Each man before him follows in sequence. Dareios' body bleeds into the tunics. And my lap is greeted with a new backside.

In the moments that follow, many of us twist the corks from our satchels. We know we should conserve what little we have. But we drink anyway.

* * *

I simply cannot weave the words I need to describe the horror of my surroundings. In the span of a single day, our rudderless ship has borne us to a land unfathomable.

The night has not brought respite from the day's unbridled heat. The air outside, though cool, is perfectly still. It does not enter the gaps and fissures in the planks. The moisture, forced from the waterlogged wood by the sun's rays, is now a thick vapor.

Our sweat runs freely, falling into the soggy tunics at our feet. Our water is gone.

Some men, parched beyond tolerance, beyond regard for decorum, wrap the tips of their cocks in cloth and piss into their hands so they can drink.

Others, who likely disobeyed our orders to fast for the day before our mission, have soiled themselves, adding more foulness to the already rank air.

I feel myself fading. My legs succumb to the constant burn. My stomach churns, threatening to empty itself with every breath. I search my body and mind for reserves. I return empty-handed.

My vision blurs and I clench my eyelids so hard my face begins to tremble.

I open them to find the cabin expanding—the walls bowing out, changing color and shape. Fat marble columns explode into the chamber from beneath and rise hundreds of feet to meet a golden dome above. Soft white light pours into the space, framing a sliver of black. A figure.

* * *

She glides towards me from across the great hall, feet soundless on the gleaming marble. The light flooding in from behind renders her as a shadow.

She nears, her form taking shape. Her soft perfect curves gently rise, fall, sway. Her impossibly long hair is alive in her wake, waving, rippling.

I wait for her in a pool of water, my lower half hidden by the hot mist dancing on the surface. My thirst and hunger are gone. So too is the fire in my thighs and calves.

She reaches the edge and emerges from the shadows. I find myself speechless at the sight of so much beauty.

Her feet disappear into the writhing steam. Faint ripples leave her tanned calves, cross the pool, find my waist, stir my loins. Descending deeper, she comes to me.

Her hands cup my face, draw it to hers. Our lips meet, part, and meet again, her tongue working at mine. Perfume rising from her breasts steals the strength from my legs.

She guides me to the edge of the pool. I feel the cool marble lip at my back as I recline. Her hands leave my face, trace the lines of my neck, my shoulders, chest and stomach. They dip into the pool to ready me.

She rises and descends. She gives me a moment to feel. To revel.

This is how it feels to be a hero, I muse. To be immortalized in couplets and choruses. To be desired by a beauteous, divine creature.

I wrap my arms around her waist and drive my hips into hers.

* * *

An elbow jabbed into my ribs wrenches me from ecstasy, thrusts me back into the nightmare of the cabin. The soldier before me is not pleased at my pulse and pressure against his rear. Or at the slick of spittle trickling down his back.

All noise from without has now ceased. The sentries have long since completed their watch. The city is asleep. The cabin has dimmed, the beams of moonlight gone, lost in a newly clouded sky. The torchlight has waned to a bloody glow.

It takes time for my eyes to adjust. When they do, they fix on my commander.

"Warriors," he says, his voice a heavy whisper. "It is time."

With his words the cabin comes to life. The soldiers emerge from cocoons of stillness. After holding our cramped positions for so long, we move stiffly and deliberately. Joints pop and crunch as we sigh with pain and relief.

The commander gives his orders. Halfway down the cabin, four soldiers crouch out of sight, sliding bronze bolts out of place and releasing the latches they'd clamped when we'd started this mission. Ten others line up along each of the belly walls and push. The flanks open, groaning on sets of hidden hinges. When the openings are wide enough, two men slip a pair of short, heavy beams in place to keep them slightly aloft.

The cool clear air rushes into the vacuous cabin as if blown by a wild gale. The foul smells fade as the temperature falls. We fill our lungs.

One by one the soldiers, bow to stern, deftly make their way out of the cabin, descending the ropes.

The moment seems unreal. Bodies glow red in the guttering torchlight. No one hesitates or stops to consider. One by one, we disappear.

When my time comes, rain patters on the beast's wooden back.

Rain, softly falling on the stones below.

The Magdeburg Incident

Story by:
M.E. Brines

Illustration by:
Morland Gonsoulin

The embassy was darkened, only one light showing in the pre-dawn gloom. I returned the salute of the guard at the gate.

"The captain's been looking all over for you, sir," he said. "He told me to have you report to him at once whenever you got back."

"Thank you, Sergeant."

I mulled whether I should report immediately or change my clothes. A quick glance showed my uniform wasn't stained. I hadn't completely disgraced myself, unlike Alexi. I did up a couple of wayward buttons and ran my hand through my hair, then hurried up to his room. No sense putting off the inevitable.

I knocked at the door. A tiny crack of light shone beneath.

"Sub-lieutenant Bryce?"

"Yes, sir."

"Well, don't stand there lollygagging. You've kept me up quite late enough as it is. Get in here."

"Yes, sir."

Captain Stephenson was wearing a nightshirt and sitting in a leather wingback chair reading a book. He laid the book on the table beside him.

"War has been declared," he announced.

"Yes, sir. The Germans declared war on the Russians three days ago. I think there was something about it in the papers."

"Don't get smart with me, Sub-lieutenant. I don't happen to care if your father is the richest man in England, or that he pulled strings in the foreign office to get you posted here."

"That wasn't my idea, sir. I volunteered for submarine duty."

"Whatever for? Those tiny little boats are filthy. They've hardly any crew."

"Exactly, sir. With only two or three officers I'm that much closer to my own command. And besides, they're the future, sir."

"The future? A boat designed to sink is absurd at best. If you want the future you should have had the Duke use his influence to get you into the aether flotilla. Those flying ships seem all the rage with the young lads these days. But such technological jiggery-popery does not impress me. When I was your age Royal navy meant ships that floated on water, not air. This Tesla coil contra-gravity business is an affront to nature, if you ask me."

"Yes, sir."

"While you were out whoring about the town until the wee hours of the morning," he paused in his tirade to gesture at the clock on the mantelpiece. "Events have taken their course. Since midnight we have been at war with the German Empire."

"What?"

"They refused to evacuate their troops from Belgium and our ultimatum expired at midnight. All of Europe is now at war."

"My God, sir."

"Yes, I don't doubt your dismay. No more whoring about like a drunken dandy. You're going to have to learn to be a sailor. And to teach you that lesson, or more likely, prove to the Admiralty what a worthless scamp you are, I've pulled some strings of my own to get you a new assignment. At first light you are to report to the cruiser *Bogatyr* as His Majesty's liaison with the Russian First Aether Cruiser Squadron."

"Yes, sir. I'll be there."

"You'd better. And when you foul up this assignment, and I know you will, by God, I'll break you." He grinned like a death's head.

"Yes, sir."

"Get out of my sight, Bryce. You reek of alcohol and carnality."

"Yes, sir." I threw him a salute. He made me wait a few heartbeats before he returned it. Then I hurried off. I had a sea bag to pack. Damn Alexi and his insatiable tavern crawling. Alone I could have completed my business with Katerina and been back way before midnight.

* * *

The sun was just rising as I stood on the dock opposite *Bogatyr*. The name was painted on the bow in gold leaf and the gray paint of the hull looked fresh. The armed sailor guarding the gangplank came to attention and we exchanged salutes.

"Permission to come aboard?" I asked, in passable Russian. He turned and yelled for his superior.

A figure in officer's whites staggered out from behind the splinter shield of a deck gun, one hand furtively slipping a bottle into a pocket. He waved with the other.

The guard let me pass and I hurried up the gangplank.

"Alexi, you dog. I can't believe you're up and moving again this early."

He patted his pocket. "Like I said, we Russians have a secret weapon."

"And probably no liver."

He took me to a spare stateroom where I stashed my bag. Then I reported to the commodore.

He was a gruff gray-bearded officer who spoke not a single word of English. After a bit of saluting all round he invited me to be his guest aboard ship. Then we had to toast the efforts against our common enemy. The vodka did act as a welcome tonic to offset the effects of the night before, although before I met Alexi I hadn't made a habit of drinking this early.

Afterwards Alexi gave me a tour of the ship. The *Bogatyr* was what was called a protected cruiser. That meant it had a modicum of armor, at least sufficient to protect it from the popguns torpedo boats and destroyers carried. With a dozen six-inch caliber guns it could make mincemeat of a flotilla of smaller boats and with the anti-gravity coil invented by Nikola Tesla and perfected by my father, it could soar above any potential adversaries with heavier armaments.

Of course, the imperial German navy had their own aether fliers, Count Zeppelin having followed Thomas Edison's lead in simply appropriating Tesla's patents. The German government had ignored the resulting lawsuits in the name of "national necessity." All that meant was that both sides in this war were equipped with the same weapons: magazine rifles, machine guns, breach-loading artillery and flying aether dreadnoughts. I thought this a recipe for stalemate and massed slaughter.

Alexi didn't share my doubts.

"Willi, you just don't understand," he had told me. "The Germans are nothing but big talk and bigger mustaches. Inside they are all cowards. A real man wouldn't have to wear a helmet with a big spike on top to impress people."

But I wasn't so sure.

* * *

Nevertheless, war had begun. But the mass armies of the Tsar took time to assemble from the far corners of his immense empire. Meanwhile, the Germans struck west, swarming into neutral Belgium, hoping to defeat the French before their Russian allies could mobilize.

Enormous German guns smashed the Belgian border fortifications in a matter of hours. Then their army flooded the country. The Belgians retreated from that horde and even the British Expeditionary Force seemed unable to halt the enemy advance. The German army was so vast it took an entire day and a half for it to march through Brussels, the Belgian capital. It seemed as if the decisive battle might be fought near Paris very soon.

But at sea both sides seemed determined for the other to strike first. Days became weeks as we waited for orders to put to sea. The Russian fleet kept busy with constant drills that seemed to do little but curtail my efforts to see Katerina. Not that her father permitted her to see me anymore. Not since she'd returned home last time in the wee hours of the morning.

Finally after three weeks we received orders to put to sea. Our mission was a sweep of the Baltic down the coast as far as Riga. Fishing boats had spotted enemy warships near there and the High Command believed they might attempt a bombardment of the city. The aether cruisers *Pallada* and *Bogatyr* along with three *Bespokniny*-class aether destroyers were to scout ahead of the fleet.

* * *

August 26th dawned dank and foggy with a feeling of rain in the air. My head hurt from too much alcohol the night before. Alexi's antics in the officer's mess didn't differ much from his habits on shore and the other junior officers seemed to delight in seeing how much vodka they could force upon me. They took great amusement in my unsteadiness once I'd had a few, never realizing the more I spilled on the outside of the mess table, the less ended up inside me. My father had thought by obtaining me a posting to Russia he was doing me a favor. But he had no idea what it was doing to my liver.

I was up on the bridge to one side between the helmsman and the trimsman, peering into the gloom. The commodore was also present, complaining at length at the diminished visibility. The *Pallada* appeared and disappeared intermittently in the mist and we reduced our speed for fear of colliding with her or one of the destroyers.

About half past eight the fog began to clear. In the distance I could see a sandy island with a lighthouse. I recognized it as Odensholm. If we'd been aboard my father's yacht we would have to watch out for the nearby shoals, but flying along at a thousand meters we had no fear of running aground.

"Captain, ship dead ahead," said the helmsman.

An aether ship belching coal smoke from its four stacks emerged from a cloudbank. A quick glance with my binoculars confirmed what I expected: the ship was flying the German naval ensign.

"Battle stations," ordered the commodore. "Hard to port, helmsman. Guns to fire when ready."

I watched as aboard the enemy ship tiny figures scrambled in response to similar orders from their commander.

Just astern of them a second ship emerged from

the fog. It was slightly smaller than the first, with only three stacks.

"Any idea of their identification, Lieutenant?" The commodore asked me.

"The first one's the *Magdeberg*, light cruiser, a dozen 4.1-inch guns, no armor. The other is probably *Augsburg* or one of her sisters, different class, same armament."

"Very good, Lieutenant."

The enemy opening fire in a near simultaneous broadside cut off further conversation. At this range it was difficult to miss, but most of their twenty-five pound projectiles merely glanced off our armor. A few slammed into our unarmored superstructure and exploded, doing unimportant damage to the unoccupied crew quarters.

Our forward turret returned fire, the two guns slovenly firing one after the other. They were followed intermittently by random shots from the other deck and casemate guns.

The Germans, probably noting our tardy response, turned and charged, black smoke belching from their funnels.

"What are they thinking?" The commodore asked. "They've crossed their own T. We can give them broadsides and only their forward guns can respond."

As if in response the *Pallada* opened a ragged broadside. The clouds behind the enemy ships erupted in black puffs.

"Commodore," I said. "They know their guns can't penetrate our armor and they're trying to close the range for a torpedo attack."

"They'll never make it."

I had my doubts but he knew his gunners. Their initial shots were wild but they quickly got the range and our much heavier hundred-pound shells began smashing into the leading enemy vessel. A huge burst of smoke and their fore funnel collapsed. Several fires broke out in her superstructure. But her forward gun continued to fire.

A German shell caromed off our forward turret and tumbled past the bridge. Splinters rattled against the armored shutters.

On their ship a black smudge from an exploding shell obscured their conning tower. Their ship began to sag from the bow. More shells slammed into it, one after another. Their guns stopped firing. The fires aboard gave off more smoke than their funnels.

Finally the ship slued to starboard and rolled sideways. Black specks fell from the deck toward the water three thousand feet below. Parachutes blossomed from a few lucky ones. Then more parachutes popped open all around her as the commander of the stricken vessel gave the order to abandon ship.

Her companion, the *Augsburg*, passed her close alongside, launching a spread of aerial torpedoes, before heeling around in a tight turn and heading away. A German destroyer making smoke to cover her retreat was surrounded by the black puffs of near misses.

Then a bright flash.

Broken in half, the severed pieces of the destroyer tumbled straight down, trailing smoke. A chance hit must have detonated a torpedo just as she was about to launch.

"Bring us about," the commodore ordered. We headed end-on into the oncoming torpedoes to minimize their chances. "Trimsman, down 100 meters, emergency rate."

The deck dropped out from under me, the commodore gambling we could fall beneath the torpedoes' path. But if the enemy had bet on us doing just that, they would have set some to run at lower altitudes.

He peered into the mist through his telescope trying to see the oncoming specks. But I saw another hazard. And an opportunity.

"Sir!" I cried. "The *Magdeberg*!" I pointed at the stricken vessel. Unmanned, it had continued to steam on in our direction, losing altitude as the steam pressure in her boilers fell, reducing the current to her Tesla coil. But our emergency dive put us on a collision course.

"Hard a port! Flank speed!"

The forward pom-pom gun barked twice and was answered by the detonation of a torpedo nearby. Two others passed harmlessly overhead.

I stepped to the rail and watched as the wreck of the *Magdeberg* slid by almost close enough to touch, headed down to a watery grave.

Or so her crew had assumed. But her present parabolic course would put her down in the shallows just off Odensholm Island. They'd abandoned ship in a hurry, maybe too much of a hurry, figuring the sea would take care of the details. But the air around was full of German parachutes and it wouldn't be long until they realized their error and took steps to correct it. I turned to the commodore.

"Sir!" I pointed to the blazing wreck of the *Magdeberg* as it passed. "You have to take a prize."

"What?"

"Send a prize crew aboard."

"It's too late for that. When it hits the water it'll just sink anyway and then we'd have to rescue the prize crew."

I glanced about. Spying a rescue locker nearby, I jerked it open, pulled out a parachute and shrugged it on.

"Then send them to rescue me."

I leaped over the side, falling toward the deck of the German ship and controlling my descent by moving my arms. I'd made a few parachute jumps from a dirigible the summer before, the same summer I'd also tried auto racing and flying lessons before deciding to join the navy. Being a wealthy playboy had its advantages, unless you wanted people to take you seriously.

I jerked the ripcord at the last second. My canopy bloomed and the straps jerked at my shoulders. But mine wasn't the only parachute in the air.

Below, the wreck of the *Magdeberg* hit the water with a tremendous splash. The broken ship taking on water settled with a list to port but couldn't actually sink because of the shallowness of the shoals.

My shoes hit the teak deck of the vessel and I shrugged out of the straps even as my canopy sagged above me. I ran toward the bridge. Enemy parachutes dotted the surrounding sea.

Scrambling up the ladder to the bridge I ignored the wreckage, and the body of the helmsman still tangled in the wheel. A small cabin behind the bridge held a nest of electronic equipment. I sorted quickly through the debris but didn't find what I sought. The radioman might have taken it with them when they abandoned ship. But there was another place it might be.

Back outside, I saw what I expected but dreaded: a German officer climbing over the rail. He was wet, drenched from his dunking in the sea, but wore a determined expression. Now it was a race.

I grabbed a fire axe from a damage control locker. Scanning the labels by the doors, I hurried down the passage. Russian was not the only language I'd picked up on my summer vacations sailing the Baltic.

It had to be here somewhere. Designers always put it close to the bridge.

There!

I tried the door. It was locked. A couple of whacks with the axe took care of that. I kicked the ruins away and stepped inside.

The room was spartan, much simpler than the Russian commodore's cabin. Pulling out the drawers of the desk revealed my prize: a thick book bound in blue leather: the *Signalbuch der Kaiserlichen Marine*, official codebook of the imperial German navy.

"Nein!"

I looked up. A sodden German in a captain's uniform confronted me over the sights of a Mauser pistol.

"Catch." I threw the big book at him. He made an attempt to catch it, but the thing probably weighed ten pounds. As he struggled with it I snatched up the axe and swung.

A moment later I stepped back out into the passage, the codebook under my arm and his pistol in my hand. I made my way to the foredeck and awaited rescue, my treasure in hand. The only person who had known it hadn't been destroyed or thrown overboard was back in his cabin with an axe in his skull. They probably wouldn't change the codes for weeks, maybe longer.

As the *Bogatyr* dropped alongside I wondered what Captain Stephenson was going to say, but thinking about it made me smile.

I didn't expect he was going be very pleased.

The Kestrel

I spied this evening gravity's bane, ground-
   Defying dusk's dirigible: an airship, soaring,
   Drifting in the dust-driven draft, mooring-
Mounted, engines churning, yearning to bound
Into the sky! Then, down, 'round, and 'round,
   As a raptor circles groundling prey, spooring,
   The *Kestrel* met the mooring, engines roaring.
Breath broken, I watched as her tether wound.

The ship's skin stretched, struts strained,
   Snapped! AND the fire that bloomed from within
Eclipsed the setting sun. Downward sparks rained,

   Fiery teardrops reflected in their salty kin.
And yet, fantasies of flight remain;
   A tragic crash shan't quash the dreams of men.

— Stace Johnson

The Skies

Steam horses glide
across the frozen, vermillion skies,
youths stand on picket fences, believing they can
fly them to escape.

Aged lowlanders grizzle,
disdainful of the brazen young,
eyes sapped by dissonance, on rocking chairs
grinding the stone verandas.

They know only Kimono servants ride the horses,
fortified skins resolute of the
shock winds.

There is an abject weariness in the plains,
obduracy in the youth that believe
the purls of steam encourage escapist thought:
on the darker curve of the sky,
the Kimonos, glide on steam horses,
respectfully collecting the
remains of the perished escapers
across the frozen vermillion skies.

— Neil Weston

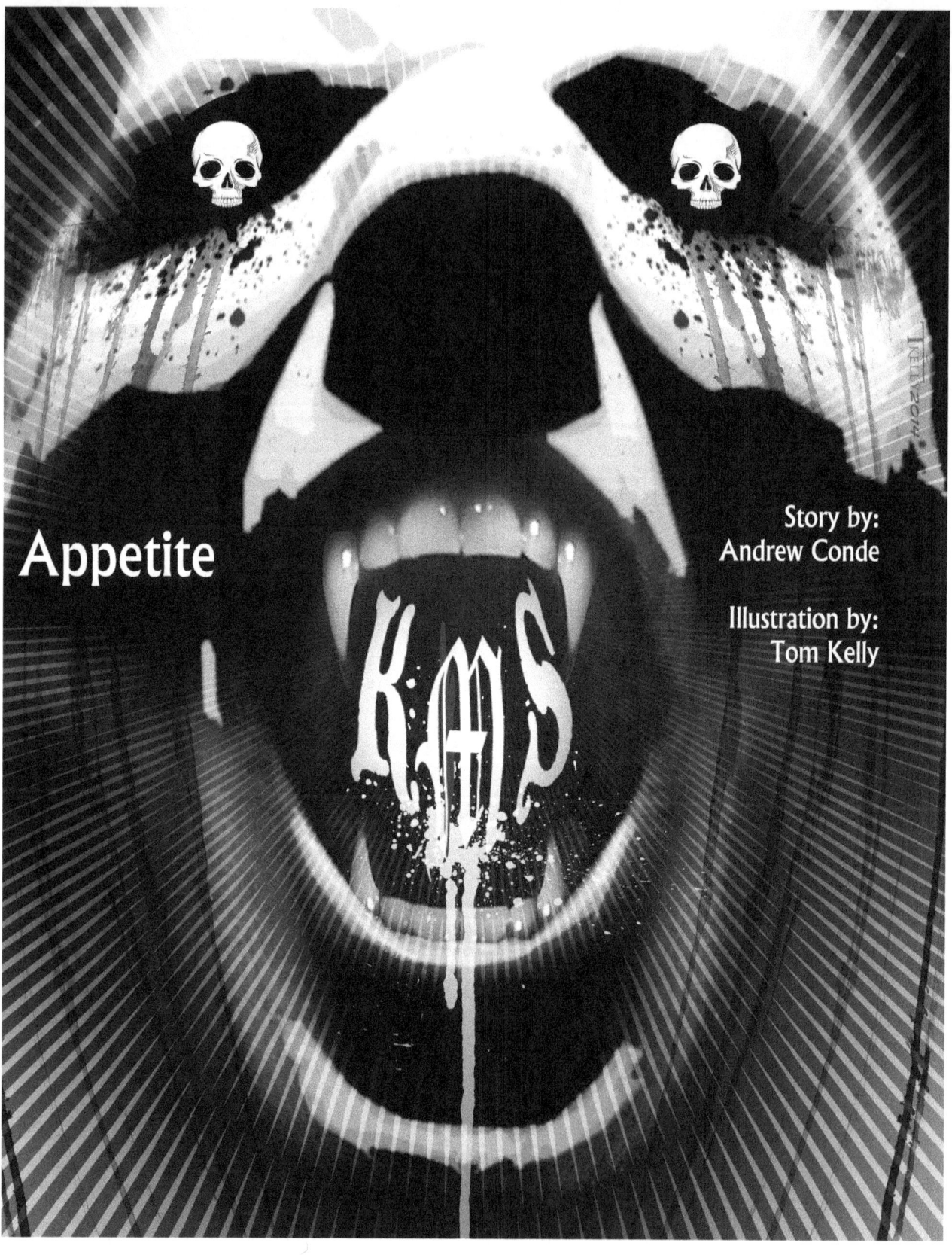

Appetite

Story by:
Andrew Conde

Illustration by:
Tom Kelly

"Aren't you a little young to go out in the ashes?" The voice wasn't deep, wasn't guttural, but still gave that impression.

Kelley glanced at the man speaking to her, and with a rueful shake of her head answered, "I go where I please."

He stepped forward, close enough to Kelley she read his name across his uniform shirt, Westerlin. "Well then, I bet it would please you to go with me. Wouldn't it?" It wasn't a question. Even without the uniform, the smell of fuel or the crease on his cheek from the ever-present air-hose, she would know him. A11 Salamanders wore the air of superiority and entitlement like an identity token.

It happened, not often, but enough. When someone saw her rounded face, her quick movements, or her confidence they would—like Westerlin—misread them as marks of youth. She didn't care. Let everyone think her young or weak, except when someone—like Westerlin—decided to capitalize on it. He grabbed her arm roughly. In a small voice, Kelley asked, "Can I wash off the soot?" Since they were next to one of the communal showers situated beside the city entrances, and since Westerlin didn't want more ash in his apartment than normal, he shoved her toward the nearest booth. She pulled the handle and let the recycled water douse her. The water tasted like ash and chemicals, but nearly everything did. Why wouldn't it? For a full mile around the city, the Salamanders burned everything. It was the only way to keep the city safe.

Westerlin gasped and Kelley knew the water did what she wanted. Burnt water rinsed the ashes form her face, revealing the keloid scar on her cheek, the sigil meaning KMS. "Oh hey, sorry, I thought you were a townie. I didn't know you were Kick."

She flicked her eyes to him and leaned back, closing her eyes dismissively. Caustics poured down, rinsing away the greasy soot, followed by more water and a final blast of warm air, just enough to dry her face. Kelley stepped from the shower and Westerlin was still there. He tried a smile, "That's the choices we have, wet or dirty, dirty or wet."

"I thought you changed your mind when you saw the scar," Kelley challenged. "Do you still think you can take me back to your place? Are you still trying to take advantage of me?"

The look that crossed Westerlin's face combined different types of fear into a single contortion. "No, that's just … I just, can I talk to you about the Kick?"

"Even though they don't hold moisture, my clothes are wet. Add to that, I'm tired, and I'm hungry," Kelley sighed. "I need to get some food in me and get home for a real shower and a nap. What do you have to say?"

"There's an Am-stat down the street, a good one. I'll show you." She found Westerlin distasteful, but a girl's gotta eat. Westerlin led the way to the Am-stat, but didn't need to do so. It was near Kelley's apartment, so of course, she knew where to go. By the time they started out, her clothes had shed all the excess moisture leaving her feeling sticky and uncomfortable. She was used to it.

The Amino-acid station served yeast-based amino-acid pabulum, the same as every Am-stat in the city, the same synthetic flavor, same small portions, and the same institutional feel. They each grabbed a bag of chewies, non-nutritional additives used to give the paste a better texture. They sat together and Kelley pulled her canteen off her belt and set it on the table.

"What's in that?" Westerlin asked.

After a long swallow from the canteen and an even longer sigh, Kelley answered, "North River water." Westerlin gaped. "'Want some?"

Of course he did. Bordering the ash-line to the north of the city, North River was one of the deadliest places on the planet and repudiated to be one of the most beautiful. Salty/sweet, the water didn't taste synthetic, didn't taste like ashes. North River water sold by the ounce and it was expensive. Westerlin forced himself to refuse, "No, I just wanted to talk to you about the Kick."

"Yeah, you said that before. First off, stop repeating yourself. Second, don't call it the Kick. We are KMS. 'Kick' makes us sound silly." She glared at him for a moment, making sure it sunk in.

"Sorry about that, sorry," Westerlin looked around and dropped his voice, almost whispering. "I want to join the KMS." If he expected to shock Kelley, he didn't. "Look, I know you guys are well-trained and get supplements and stuff. I mean, look at you. I thought you were younger, but you're just healthy. That's food, not training, and not this slop either. How do I join?"

The city held three-million, a lot for an Earth colony but not surprisingly so. Nearly five-thousand worked as Salamanders, burning back the aggressive plant life, what the humans called Carolina, leaving ashes the Blues couldn't cross. This Salamander wanted more; he wanted to face the Blues directly with the fifteen members of the KMS.

Kelley pointed over her shoulder at a mural on the

wall. "See that picture? Every Am-stat has one similar, a stylized Blue cowering from a Salamander. In the picture, you're clean and they show the Blue as the color blue, while real Salamanders wear ash and the Blues are green." He knew what a real Blue looked like, big green insects with four legs, green chitin and spines to stab through a man like blades into the pabulum they both ate. They were monsters, pure and simple. "You keep the city safe and the townies love you for it. The school-kiddies write reports about Salamanders and stage plays in your honor. KMS scares people. Is that what you want?"

"Yeah," Westerlin answered simply. She looked at him as if she didn't understand so he had to explain more. "It's not just that, you know. I wanna do more for the city. They say that if we wipe out the Blues and are the only life form left, we'll get back in contact with Earth."

"For one, there are four types of life here, Carolina, Blues, humans and yeast. For another, do you really believe that?" Kelley asked around another spoon of paste.

"Why else would they refuse contact? The enemy infested every colony they could with Blues and Earth is worried about them spreading. They shouldn't worry. They got resources and tech to clean them all out, slug-throwers and explosives and all that stuff from the history books. It's different here, but as long as they see the Blues eating humans here not there, they just quarantine us."

'Yeah, you don't seem real altruistic. You don't care about Earth politics any more than I do. We haven't spoken to anyone off-planet in decades, so we don't know what happened with the War. Who even cares?" She glanced at Westerlin, daring him to answer. "Tell me the truth, besides the scar that scares every townie in the city or the lies and exaggerations from the council, why would you want to be KMS?"

For years, Westerlin dreamed of KMS, but he never worried about explaining why. "I don't know. I guess I like the scar. People see that and just get out of the way. The Salamander uniform and the smell of fuel gets me a 'yessir' and 'nossir,' sometimes a free drink, but that's it, you know?" He paused and shrugged. "Once a week, Salamanders get a textured yeast-cake with lipid sauce. That's the big thanks from the council, but you guys get more. We kill ourselves out there until the Blues eat us, we burn to death, or worse, retire inside, too old and crippled for anything but pity. Letting a Blue pick its teeth with my bones is so much better than coughing out a lungful of ash

in the retirement apartments."

"Food and fear, huh?" Kelley asked but didn't expect an answer. "What makes you think you're qualified for KMS?"

Westerlin had no problem answering that. He bragged, "I'm strong. I'm quick. Ask anyone, they'll tell you what I'm like in a tussle. Do you think you could get me a try-out or something? They say they pick you for duty when you're kids, but I'm in really good shape."

For a long moment, Kelley considered the guy across from her, the way he first approached her, his reaction to her KMS scar, everything he said, his confidence, his arrogance, and even his obvious strength. He was in really good shape for a norm his age. "Tell you what, in two days, we go back to the North River. The Blues like to pick off the morons willing to risk their lives for a bottle of water." She took a long pull from her canteen and offered it again to Westerlin. He took it this time and drank. Kelley waited until he was done to continue. "I'll talk to the rest of the team about taking you out. We don't advertise it, but we do take people out from time to time. I'm sure they'll be happy to have you. It's a three-day trip along the river. If you don't like that, back to burning. You'll come back to the city with an adventure and a bottle of water."

"No hey, when we get back, you'll beg me to join."

"I'm sure you will be part of the KMS," she assured him. He gave her his residence number and took off.

* * *

The War: *the conflict resulting from an advanced race attacking human-occupied space. Speculation as to the alien motive is futile.*
* * *

Two days later, and Westerlin didn't think she was coming, even though he took that day and the next four off to be ready. Over the hours between his talk with Kelley and his waiting for her, even when out burning, he convinced himself back and forth that she would meet him, she wouldn't, the rest of the KMS would refuse him, or that they would celebrate him by the end of the week. He even worked up scenarios where he could save them from something terrible, or maybe survive while all the Blues ate the KMS. He would be the hero then, start the KMS new. He was in the midst of designing a new sigil when his door pinged.

In the hall stood four KMS. Westerlin looked out and smiled. Usually, a dozen townies and their children filled the hall with noise, but not with the KMS there. Oh, how he wanted to be a part of them! He almost didn't recognize Kelley. When he met her, ashes and soot covered her completely, but in the hall, her red hair glistened above pale skin and bright eyes. The other KMS, three men all had various degrees of darker skin, darker hair, but eyes that shined just as bright. "Can we come in?" Kelley asked.

Westerlin stepped back before he could even think of a reply, and the four KMS stepped inside. "Are you ready to go?"

"Well, I'm just wearing my uniform."

"That's fine," she assured him. "Our uniforms are tailor made for each of us, fireproof, waterproof, and very tough. Your uniform is about the same, only doesn't fit as well and is easier to cut."

"When do I get a weapon?"

The three KMS men tried to hide smiles, but Kelley answered, "We're not allowed to wear weapons inside the city. We'll stop at an armory on the way out."

"Do I need anything else? I have some rats from work."

"Yeah, we take our food with us. We don't need your rations," one of the KMS men said gruffly. For a moment, Westerlin thought the KMS guy was angry but realized that years of breathing ash roughened his voice just as it did for older Salamanders. The thought gave Westerlin confidence. KMS are just as human as the rest of us.

The five rode down the elevator together and headed out in the street. He thought he understood the power the scar represented, but in the middle of a clutch of KMS, Westerlin noticed how differently the townies treated them. People literally ran when they saw the KMS, hid in dark doorways, or just cowered as far from them as possible. Westerlin reveled in it, but the KMS didn't even notice. They walked a while to the edge of town and the nearest doorway. The spotters guarding the door talked through the grille, one on the outside, the older keeping his eyes on the ashes while the one inside waited to raise the alarm. Being intent as much on the conversation as the possibility of approaching Blues, neither spotted the arriving group.

The gravelly voiced KMS, Chidden, announced, "Let us out," and laughed at the boy struggling with the door's release. "Calm down little fella."

"I need to be more vigilant," the guard explained, making Chidden laugh some more.

Chidden explained. "Hey, if you look this direction,

you won't see the Blues outside. I'd rather a human sneak up on you than one of them. Now, if you don't mind, we need to go out in the ashes."

The KMS donned their smoked goggles and ash filters as they stepped from the tenebrous city, past the guards, through the wall and out into the ashes. Chidden and Kelley led the way with Westerlin following and the other two KMS behind. They got to a hut between two of the city doors and opened it to see the rest of the KMS waiting. Kelley introduced Westerlin, "Guys, this is Westerlin. He wants to be KMS more than anything." Some of the KMS looked up, but most concentrated on their preparations.

"What are they doing?" Westerlin asked.

Kelley looked at him as if he was stupid, but decided to explain anyway. "Making weapons. We have the glassworks cast us sheets and we knap out our blades. Metal costs too much and wouldn't last anyway. Let the council use any iron they get in our supplements; glass makes better blades."

"I thought you guys had slug-throwers and stuff."

A few of the KMS chuckled at that. Kelley explained, "Nobody carries a gun outside of the council. Seriously, a Blue won't notice a wound from one of those. With the glass, we can open them up and spatter blue ichor everywhere." She went on to explain the different styles of blades the KMS used, the thin shards designed with a primitive airfoil but that they rarely threw, the long blades used more for hacking plant-life than killing, and the small triangular blades they tied to their clubs, the favored weapon of the KMS.

"What are the clubs made of?" Westerlin asked.

"Human femurs blackened with ash," Chidden laughed. "The Carolina doesn't grow anything worthwhile and the Blues skeletons are brittle chitin. What else could we use? Don't look so horrified. Every single one of our clubs came from a former member of the KMS, that way they can be part of us forever."

Kelley laughed at the look on Westerlin's face and directed him over to the unprocessed glass. He couldn't help with the actual knapping, since it was a skill that took longer to master than they had to wait, so she had him sort glass into three piles. It was all green and thick, but chunks of different sizes needed to go in different piles. After an hour of that, Westerlin's hands bled and boredom weighed on him like a pile of ash.

Without warning, the KMS came to life, all standing in unison and turning to the door. "It's time to go," Kelley announced. She quickly wrapped Westerlin's hands in bandages, handed him a long blade, and two throwers. "Basically, you need to just watch and try not to get in anybody's way. If a Blue gets too close, slash it with the long. If someone needs the throwers, we'll take them from you. Don't worry; today will be in the ash and along the river."

"What about tomorrow?" Westerlin asked, but she had already stepped outside and donned her smoked goggles. Westerlin grabbed a set of the goggles and awkwardly strapped them around his head.

Next to the shack, a pile of ashen-grey bags of supplies waited for the KMS. Westerlin hurried to keep up, but the KMS waited for him to grab the last pack and heft it over his shoulder. It wasn't as heavy as he expected.

Over in the distance, they saw a group of Salamanders burning back the plants the humans learned to hate. Inedible, unusable, the green and yellow Carolina weed grew fast enough to necessitate constant monitoring, constant burning lest it approach the city. Any bit of it could hide the Blues, so every bit of it needed to be destroyed. Even without the Blues, Carolina would soon engulf the city, so until the humans could come up with a defoliant, Salamanders had to burn.

Sixteen people trudged through the ashes, the KMS and Westerlin, and for twenty minutes, silence surrounded the group. Almost as a miracle, they topped a rise to see the river spread out before them. He'd seen it before, but the river still took Westerlin's breath away. One bank was grey and black ash, the other bright green Carolina twisting and shuddering as it grew with a thin strip of glossy water dividing them. The KMS slid down the bank and into the water, as if they belonged there. Kelley looked at Westerlin and asked, "Don't you want to come down?" For an answer, he slid through the ash and fell heavily in the water. "Oh yeah, that's right. The council tells you Salamanders that you cannot approach the river. They think you'll contaminate it." She looked over at one of the KMS urinating in the water and laughed.

"Don't they monitor you guys?" Westerlin asked.

"Why would they?" one of the KMS replied, a woman named Kaidee. "As long as we do our jobs, they look the other way. Burke, what happened when you broke that guy's arm for spilling your chewies?" Burke wasn't really listening but his shrug was enough answer. "Exactly, they didn't do anything. We had a guy who flipped out once and killed a handful of townies. Nobody cares what we do, as long as we kill Blues as we do it. They set these laughable quotas.

How could they ever check if we kill the allotted fifty Blues a week?"

Kelley added, "Or that we usually wipe out three times the quota? As long as they don't find out what we're really doing out here, they won't have unrealistic expectations."

Westerlin asked, "But if you kill so many Blues, why don't you tell them?" Kelley and Kaidee both just shrugged, the standard KMS answer. "Do you think you could ever wipe them out?"

Chidden growled, "That's what we're supposed to do out here, but the council won't train enough of us. They say the augments and the Mendelex are too expensive, but they're just scared. If thirty of us could wipe out an entire planet of Blues, they're afraid that twenty of us might decide to stage a coup."

"What kind of person would want that?" Kaidee laughed.

* * *

Blues: A genetically modified insectoid race planted on Earth colonies during the War. Photosynthetic, attack humans on sight. Named for their blue ichor.

* * *

They chatted for a while longer, insulting the council, the Salamanders and especially the townies, when Burke, the KMS who looked most in danger of falling asleep and floating down the river, jumped up and grabbed his club. Westerlin had no idea what made him jump, but it hit the other KMS just as fast. Sopping wet, the KMS grabbed their weapons and bristled with anxious enthusiasm.

Westerlin didn't even notice the Blue that attacked him until the copper-based ichor splashed across his chest. Kelley laughed at his expression of horror. "You gotta watch out for them!" The laugh made him feel impotent, but the Blues moved so fast, a green streak amongst the green.

The KMS killed several Blues while Westerlin stood there, his freshly filled canteen open in his hand and blue ichor still dripping off him. In the silence that followed, the KMS waited to see if more Blues were coming, but didn't wait long. They resumed their playing in the water as if nothing happened.

"I didn't even move," Westerlin announced. Kelley shrugged. "It's the training right? That's how you do what you do."

"You better wash off that blood," she advised. "There are incompatible proteins in there that could make you sick. Rinse out your canteen too." Westerlin did as she told him. "There were only six Blues, a scout group. They patrol the ash line and jump anyone they see."

With a strange sense of pride washing over him simply from being there, Westerlin bragged, "They're going to go hungry today."

"Blues don't eat humans," Kelley chided. "That's a baseless rumor. We can't eat them, and they can't eat us. It's an incompatible protein thing again. Come on, we're moving out. Lots of hours left."

The KMS climbed the bank of the river into the Carolina, whacking tangles that reared up quicker than any plant should move. In a few minutes, they were deep in the Carolina with their back trail covered as soon as they stepped away, as if they were never there. The world around them was green, an undulating mass of writhing Carolina, hiding the contours of the planet. Every rustle of the Carolina brought Westerlin's blade up, but it was just the growing, the constant motion of the plant. The sun lowered in the sky and the KMS took off their goggles and ash filters, trudging through the deepening dark, the green-tinted night of the land outside the ash line.

"Aren't we going to set up camp?" Westerlin asked. Kelley hushed him with a touch. Full night and the wind picked up, rustling the leaves. Westerlin had never smelled wind without ash.

"The Rock!" a voice cried from the front of the group, eliciting a collective sigh. "Who has the fuel?" Westerlin expected a conflagration as the KMS cleared an area for their camp. Instead, it was a little fire on a small scrap of bare rock. The KMS cut back the area around the fire and settled in around it.

"Is this camp?"

"Sure, the Carolina makes a great bed once the fire's out. It won't grow without light. Besides, Blues don't move after dark, so we're safe that way too. This is the only good spot for a long way, a big rock to keep the fire from spreading, and if you'll notice, there's a cliff-face above us to keep out the weather."

"I don't see anything."

Even knowing that Westerlin couldn't see it, Kelley shrugged. She explained, "The Mendelex makes our eyes more light-sensitive. That started as a side-effect, but once we figured out that Blues don't move at night, we centered most of our strategy on visual cues."

Chidden growled at Kelley, "So, what's the plan, Chief?"

Kaidee corrected him, "'We're going for a hive, remember? That means Sweet gets the honor."

Sweet was the tallest KMS by a long shot, but with the same rounded features and graceful movement.

He stepped to the fire and breathed in the smell of burning Carolina. A collapsible pot of water near the fire added a slight fog to the light around his face, but he relished it as much as the smoke. "If that's the plan, we need to hurry up and get to bed. Last time we went for a hive, it was in the valley, but we got a report of one along the river, some Salamander spotter. We head back to the river and see if we can find it. A hive along the river guarantees more deaths than one anywhere else can boast. A few days ago, a Salamander group lost 35% of their guys. Did you hear about that Salamander?"

Westerlin answered, "Yeah. The bodies were pretty messed up, but we got them all back. Salamanders don't leave out dead for the Blues."

Sweet agreed, "Commendable, but beside the point. The water is a big draw. If that many Salamanders doornail, then that means a good 15-20 water-runners a week at least. The council won't let the townies know that the Blues don't move at night, so the morons think that daylight is safer."

"He led our last hive attack," Kelley explained. "Whoever is most qualified for whatever we're doing is the leader of whatever we're doing. The council insists on a hierarchy, but our way works better. We tell them that Evangeline is our boss because she deals with them better than the rest of us. I run the river patrols. Geodesy works our valley patrols. Every KMS eventually finds himself or herself a niche."

"All fifteen of you are experts?" Westerlin asked incredulously.

"Not really. Kaidee and Dell alternate our ambush sites, stuff like that. When we doornail, someone has to take over, and the training takes a while."

Chidden took over for Kelley's explanation, "The training takes seven years, and the latest noob is two years out. By the time she can join us, I bet we're down to six."

'You got it!" Kaidee cried. "I'll take that bet. Lake is less than eighteen months from joining, and she looks quick."

"Besides," Kelley added, "We have Westerlin here to keep us in shape until Lake graduates." The KMS involved in the conversation laughed but Westerlin still felt confused.

Kaidee changed the subject by announcing, "Water's boiling."

From the packs they carried, the KMS took out small packages of dehydrated texturized yeast protein they used as rations, the same yeast-cake with lipid sauce the council used as treats for the Salamanders.

They all dug in, and when Westerlin finished, Kelley handed him another package. He ate that one too and fell back in the Carolina, fuller than he'd ever been. Kelley laughed and flopped down beside him.

Kelley offered, "Sleep as deep as you can. We get up at dawn and head out. If you aren't up by full daylight, the Carolina will cover you."

That comment did not help Westerlin in his sleep. He woke several times during the night with images of the ugly plant growing out of his nose stuck in his mind. He fell back asleep the last time only to have Kelley wake him. "It's time." To Westerlin, the morning had yet to begin, but to the KMS any light at all meant the Blues could move, the Carolina could grow, and that was enough to get them out of camp. The KMS turned to Kelley who set them in formation to head back to the river. They would follow it up to the hive where Sweet would take over. Long blades out and swinging, the returned to the river, splashed about for a few minutes, refilled their canteens, and continued off.

They stopped for refreshment several hours later. Westerlin stepped to the middle of the group and found Kelley sitting on the carcass of a dead Blue, the copper of its blood staining the Carolina with color and the air with scent. "Where did you find that?"

The KMS who heard looked at Westerlin for a moment before shrugging almost in unison. Kelley sighed and explained, "Charlock is on point with Burke. One of them must have spotted it. Single Blues are stupid and easy to kill. I guess for you, any Blue is a big deal. We only get excited when we find a clutch. The hive of course is another matter entirely."

"They say the Blues are smart," Westerlin offered between bites of his yeast-cake. He couldn't believe how many of the savory meals they carried nor how freely they distributed them to him. "I mean, they're bugs, right? I can't imagine any brains."

"They have a hive-mind," Kelley explained. "The more of them together, the smarter they are. I don't think you've ever seen any of the bigger ones, the drones. They stay around the hives as protection, eight-foot at the shoulder, twelve legs as big around as my thigh. One of them stabs you, you won't even feel it, and they're a bitch to kill, tough. From what we figure, they are all pretty mindless individually, only smart in groups except the queen. Not many of us have even seen a queen, only Geodesy, Chidden, Charlock and Evangeline."

Sweet volunteered, "I don't ever want to see one." Kelley shrugged at that. "There's a queen in every hive, but it's difficult to get to them."

Chidden announced, "The queen I saw was beautiful. A huge shiny copper color speckled with red. I thought it was blood at first, but they actually have that as coloration. You don't ever want to find a hive during daylight. We lost eight KMS before we could get away, two more that night when we returned. This is the first year we've had a full contingent in a long time."

Suddenly, as one, the KMS stood and started out again. They didn't seem concerned about the Blues, only about getting further along the river. Westerlin found himself again in the middle of the group, where he still twitched at the slightest unidentified sound, but no matter how alert, he wasn't ready for the Blues. This time, a larger group came out of the Carolina and attacked the KMS. With reflexes tuned by training and the Mendelex, the KMS moved faster than the Blues, almost faster than Westerlin could see. They killed four Blues before the creatures scored their first mortal blow. Westerlin saw the green leg striped with black lash out and punch its way through Burke's head in gory reminder of his dream, a shaft of green out a man's bleeding face. When Westerlin started screaming, Evangeline knocked him down and kicked him in the chest hard enough to knock the wind out of him and shut him up. The Blues blended too perfectly with the Carolina for the KMS to allow devaluation of any other sense. Westerlin sat up to see the rest of the fight but closed his eyes quickly. He knew better than to allow the screams behind his teeth to escape, but if the fight lasted long enough, he knew someone would hit him again. It didn't.

In moments, one KMS and eighteen Blues lay dead around them. "Bad day," Chidden announced. There was nothing more for anyone to say, so they slid down the bank and into the river, hoping to wash off the blood, the blue and the red.

"I don't think I'm cut out for this," Westerlin whispered but Kelley still heard him. She simply shrugged and bandaged a vicious wound on her arm.

"Casualties?" Evangeline asked. She took note of Burke, the wounds that several KMS sported, and the damage to one of their pots. The council would complain about that the most. They planned on replacing the KMS members regularly, but the equipment was added expense they didn't want. Westerlin had no blood on him, but washed in the river anyway. Kelley added the contents of Burke's pack to Westerlin's pack. He didn't say anything about it, didn't care. All he wanted was to get through the day and go back home. He might even quit the Salamanders after that. The Blues terrified him in ways they never did before.

* * *

KMS: *Kelion-Monte Statute, law giving security groups autonomy. Also known as the Kick Murder Squad.*

* * *

Night fell again, and the fifteen found another spot to make a new camp. "There aren't very good rocks here, but the Carolina burns too quickly for safety without a cairn of some sort. This pile works." Kelley helped Westerlin to sit. "You're in a little shock. Why don't you just stay here while we make dinner? Would some food do you any good?" Westerlin didn't respond.

Charlock asked, "'Who carries the new clubs?"

That woke Westerlin up. "That's not right. You people aren't right. Do you know what you look like when you fight those things? I can't tell the difference! Blood and Carolina covered all of you Blues and KMS, fighting silently and horribly. Even your weapons are the same color! And now you butcher one of your own so you can have more weapons!"

"Control your boy Kelley," Chidden commanded.

Westerlin didn't notice. "I'm going back to the city. As soon as it's daylight, I'll make my way south."

Kelley shrugged. "If that's what you want; good luck with that. Blues sleep at night and patrol during the day. We're about fifteen miles from the city now, so the chances of you making it all the way back are pretty slim. Can't find the city by night; can't pass the Blues by day."

"I can't be one of you."

Chidden shrugged, "Sure you can," and lunged forward with a shard of glass to slash across Westerlin's cheek. Westerlin turned to run and Kelley caught him another slash. He fell, and Kelley landed on top of him, carving the rest of the KMS sigil in his face.

"Please," Westerlin cried. "I can't be one of you." The KMS shrugged almost in unison. "I'll die and you'll make me into weapons."

"Too late now," Kelley said clirnbing off him. "You wanted, you asked, and now, you got." She looked over her shoulder to the fire. "How's Burke?"

Someone from the fireside called back, "Almost ready."

A revolting smell impinged on Westerlin's self-pity. "What is that?"

"Burke," Kelley explained.

"Oh, don't tell me…" Westerlin gasped. "Is that why you brought me? Is it? If he hadn't died, you'd have … I'm going to die tomorrow." He fell to the ground, knowing he could not escape, knowing that the marks on his face guaranteed him staying with the KMS, even if only for the moment, even if they only had one use for him. Actually two, since they always needed new clubs as well as the protein, and both had to come from a member of the KMS.

Kelley shrugged and motioned Westerlin to join her for her meal. She still found Westerlin distasteful, but a girl's gotta eat.

Horrible toothache
Microscopic aliens
Mine zinc from fillings

— William Landis

A Night at the Club

Story by Ian Brazee-Cannon
Illustration by Teresa Tunaley

The breeze tosses a potato chip wrapper across the parking lot as I approach the door. The sun had set a short while ago and now the pieces are gathering within the chosen game board. It was my turn to choose our gaming arena and after years of scouting, this one felt the most promising. These 'dance clubs' are intriguing places. So much energy being generated and such unique playing pieces gathered every night.

I enter the establishment.

It is early in the evening. The crowd is still light. The band is finishing up the sound check.

I station myself at a secluded table that has a clear view of most of the club and the whole of the dance floor.

I wait for my opponent to arrive. It will give me time to take notes of the playing pieces and start work on my strategy.

From my table I watch as the pieces enter the game board.

The band is on stage. There are four members. Each of them wears an outfit that is stylized from a well-known musician. The inspirations are from four distinct bands of four varying musical styles. This conflict of appearance gives a sense of disconnect before the music begins.

As the band starts to play, a crowd of dancers gathers in front of the stage. These are the playing pieces.

I can already feel the energies the crowd is producing. Every emotion, each little reaction, the dancing and the music and so much more: each generates a unique energy unnoticed by most beings. These energies flow around the room, mixing and conflicting on a level that affects living things in a manner most are unaware of.

Just as the playing pieces are unaware of us, the game players, and our manipulations.

Most noticeable on the dance floor is an older lady, most likely the eldest patron in the club. Her shoulder length hair is artificially white. In what seems to be a desperate attempt to be noticed, her blouse and floor length skirt are as white as her hair. Her outfit is completed with a white scarf that she flings around carelessly as she dances. Due to her bulky figure she resembles a giant snowball, bouncing around within the crowd. She is a white blotch moving through a crowd of dark figures.

As she gets close to the stage, the lady in white makes flirtatious glances towards the lead guitarist. He smiles politely at her, but seems more interested in playing to the younger women in the crowd.

An Asian man stumbles off the dance floor, clearly having had too much to drink already. He is clean shaven and dressed in clothing that was 'in fashion' a decade ago. His shirt is a size too large, resting loose on his frame. Only half of the buttons are done, so his chest is revealed frequently as he moves.

A waitress is rushing around tending to the patrons who are gathered at the tables. Her long brown hair is tied up in what is referred to as 'ponytails'. The wide rimmed glasses she wears fit with the 'librarian' look. As with the other young ladies who work here, she is wearing a form fitting t-shirt and a skirt that goes halfway to her knees. Every so often she sneaks in a quick dance as she goes about her duty.

Making an endless trek from dance floor to tables and back again is a young lady who is attracting a large amount of attention from the men and even a few women as she passes. Their interest is in her blouse. It is transparent, revealing her black lace bra clearly to all who wish to look. Outside of certain social requirements, there seems little point to her wearing this piece of clothing.

The owner of the establishment is making his rounds. He is a large man, well dressed and professional in his appearance. He does not hesitate to stop and speak with anyone he passes. He cracks a few jokes and laughs in good humor at other's jokes. There is a sense of charm in his smile. As he journeys around the room his strides are confident and he radiates an aura of control. There is no doubt this is his place.

And those are just a handful of the potential playing pieces here this evening. The club is full with a wide variety of individuals. The game tonight is already building up to be quite stimulating.

As I am examining the crowd I sense her entrance.

My opponent has arrived.

I look around to see her noticing me. As she makes her path to my table I know she is taking in the crowd and picking out the pieces that interest her.

I stand and greet her as she approaches.

"Greetings," I say. "What do you think of the game board?"

"Lots of possibilities here," she replies. "It should make for a substantial game."

There is something about her voice that bothers me.

"Is something upsetting you?"

"We have been on this world a long time now and I am wondering if that has been a wise choice."

"Do you grow tired of this world then?"

"It came to me that it might be beneficial for us both to move into other arenas in order to get noticed and gain rank within the community."

"Something to think about."

There is a pause between as we both contemplate this idea.

I break the silence.

"Shall we begin then?"

"Yes, I am ready."

"Then as this was my choice of game board, you are granted the first move."

No time is wasted as she makes her opening move.

* * *

So there we sit for hours as the game goes on. The energies of the room alter with every move, more often than not in small variances that only she and I can feel. Every so often one of us makes a larger move that even the humans notice, yet are prone to write it off as being nothing to pay attention to.

I make a move and the white lady's scarf is flung into the face of a man behind her, making him stumble with his pick up line. The young lady he has been moving in closer and closer to, laughs.

It is her turn to make a move and the Asian man realizes he has spilled alcohol on his shirt and rushes off to the restroom. In his rush, he trips up the waitress, but she is quick and no drinks are spilled.

There is a slap from across the room. A couple gets so caught up in their passion they forget they are in a public place. A man's pants are ripped by the loose nail in the wall behind him. A young lady stumbles around in a drunken haze. Several men are eyeing her. The owner escorts her to a barstool and instructs one of his employees to keep an eye on her. A drink is knocked over, causing a young lady to rush off to the restroom. A man coughs up a peanut that he had not fully chewed before swallowing.

And so the game goes as the tide of victory swings back and forth between us.

A young dark-skinned man enters the dance floor. He approaches a young lady. He trips up just before he reaches her. In the confusion he finds himself face to face with a different young lady. In his over confidence he starts his flirtation with his new target. This ends when the lady's girlfriend appears and drags her away. The man turns to find the young lady he originally had targeted is now engaged with a different young man.

"The Kwal-Tik gambit? You've not used that

since England, two hundred and twenty three years ago," I say.

"Still an effective move," she replies.

We both feel the changes in the energies. She has gained a fair lead now. I was foolish. She caught me off guard and now I will need to be creative to keep myself in the game. Good for me that I kept one piece out of the game so far.

The lady with the transparent blouse reappears. She has been outside engaged in various activities with some friends.

She walks to the center of the dance floor. She is energetic with her moves. A crowd is drawn to her. I prepare for the final part of my move...

A string on the bass guitar snaps. Other members of the band react to this, as they try to not let it stop the show. The music is now off beat just slightly. The atmosphere on the dance floor has changed.

I look to my opponent. She has a puzzled look on her face.

"You did not make that move," I say as a statement.

"Nor did you," she replies.

Without another word the game is put on pause as we search the room.

Standing off to the side of the bar, at the area all patrons enter the main club area from, is an older man. He is clearly one of us. He is watching us and most likely has been for some time, but as we were caught up in the game we did not sense him.

I give a motion with my hands to signal him to join us.

He walks through the crowd without any change in his pace, despite the constant motion of people.

My opponent and I stand as he nears the table.

"Greeting," she says to him. "By your move, I am taking it that you are interested in joining our game."

"If it is not too much a hassle," he replies.

"Please, take a chair and join us," I say.

I watch him as he finds an empty chair and I notice that his movements are not as fluid as his walking was.

"First time on Earth?" I ask as he returns to the table.

"Yes," he answers. "I heard that there were games of worth to be found by those who played here. I am always looking for new arenas to play in."

Over the centuries many other players have come by Earth to play a game or two with us. In the end my regular opponent and I have been the only two to find consistent enjoyment in the game boards found here.

"These creatures are of too basic a design," our new player says. "They would not be my normal choice for playing pieces."

"I find there to be a fair amount of complexity to them," I reply. "They also have such a wide range of energy to produce."

Our third player nods in interest.

"Back to the game then," my regular opponent says.

Our mutual silence is all the agreement needed.

* * *

Now the game resumes with a third player. I feel sorry for the new comer. He has come very late into our game and I doubt he will be able to catch up as we were near concluding for the night. For although his surprise move did upset both of our game plans, a good player always has multiple strategies in play and can switch from one to another quickly.

As moves are made the game is drastically altered. Many of our old moves are now irrelevant and best forgotten as the game advances into new areas. I am satisfied to see that I am taking a good lead. My regular opponent is not adapting to our third player very well. I am confident that I can achieve victory in short order.

Now for our third player to make a move.

The Asian man has had more alcohol and is barely able to stay on his feet. He tries to take a seat on a barstool, but slips and falls to the floor. As he tries to get up, his foot slips out and trips the woman in white, who is trying to return to the dance floor after relieving herself.

She fights to keep on her feet, stumbling a fair distance. She catches herself on the bar. In doing so she flings an empty glass through the air.

The glass lands heavy on the table were the lady in transparent clothes is sitting with friends. The shattering of the glass startles all at the table. The lady jumps from her chair. Her shirt gets caught in the chair and is torn to uncover her lacey bra.

I am unable to stop from laughing at the sight of her being embarrassed about her new predicament when there is truly little change in what everyone around can see of her.

As the lady and one of her friends rush off to the lady's room, the owner emerges from a back room. Behind him I see the young lady who had had too much to drink earlier. She is pulling her shirt back on.

The owner asks the waitress what is going on.

The waitress has been checking on the lady in white. She gives a quick rundown of what she saw.

The owner is not happy and starts giving orders. The young lady slips past him and vanishes into the club.

Another staff person has moved over to clean up the broken glass.

Several other members of the staff are helping the Asian man to his feet.

The room is filled with confusion at this point. All energies are altered now. The game has been changed drastically with the one move.

I realize that I had underestimated the new player's skills.

We both give him a curious look as we move on with the game.

I see that there is little hope of winning now. That one move has upset the playing field and left me and my regular opponent with little hope of victory.

* * *

Our game is played to the end. I am unable to regain any noticeable headway. In the end the newcomer wins the game, despite his late start.

As the game ends all three of us stand as one, following the custom. My original opponent and I nod to our third player to officially concede the game.

"A well played game," I say.

"Thank you," he replies. "I find this locale intriguing with the possibilities for future observations. Regretful that it is time to destroy it."

My regular opponent exchanges a look with me. His statements help make it clear as to why we lost. The defeat is now truly a learning experience, not at all reflecting negatively on our skills as players.

"I suspected you were a Master..."

"Grand Master actually."

"A Grand Master of the old style."

"We are honored not only to have been privileged to get play a match with you, but to be given such a perfect lesson on over confidence."

"However, we do not play by the rules of the Nast'Vallo mandate."

"Instead we play by the revised protocols. We symbolically destroy the game board and agree to refrain from playing that location ever again."

The Grand Master gives a disappointed exhale.

"As I suspected. More and more players are abandoning the old ways out of sympathy for the pieces. For good or ill the game is changing. I await the future to see if this is an improvement or the death of the games."

"I see it as leaving the game board so others may find it and be allowed the joy of playing the game that is there."

The Grand Master looks at me, smiles and gives a nod of approval.

"Well said. I look forward to returning to this world at some point and engaging in another game with you two. You both showed promise and talent this evening. I shall be keeping a watch as to where you both go from here."

With that the Grand Master bows and walks away.

I am left with my normal opponent. I catch her in a moment of contemplation. Most likely she is pondering the Grand Master's compliment.

"Until our next match then?" I ask.

"Until that time," she replies.

"As it is your turn to choose the game board, I am interested to see just what manner of locale you decided upon."

"I have some ideas, " she says. "I shall attempt to take less than a decade in making the choice this round."

We both bow and take our leave of one another.

I am sure that tonight's game has given her many new ideas of future strategies. Our matches to come should be far more challenging.

They are challenges I am greatly looking forward to.

The River

A deep river flows by the mage's tower.
The water, gray, green and yearning for the sea,
Gropes at the foundations with swirling fingers.
Stone is patient.
The mage's woman dips her bucket into the course;
She is weeping again.
The river catches her tears and knows
Water is more patient than stone.
Frogs call the rain;
The tide, though distant, hears all water.
The moon whispers it.
Night pours down from an unseen shroud,
Lifting the river above the reeds
To the tower stones, cold as the mage's heart.
The river does not respond to words, gestures
Or sigils.
It cradles the woman's boat
Like a womb,
Rising, falling, spinning her away
From the echoes of the tower's fall.

— F.T. McKinstry

Ode to Yon Glizan Orbs, or No?
(after John Keats)

You, still untrammeled just beyond our scopes?
You, 20,000 light years from our home,
dwarf of red yet giant within our hopes,
far beyond our own celestial dome.
What is it about you that draws us nigh?
Alien or human, we know not which
inhabitants you'll be, but we shall find
a way to fold time and space, make a stitch
and thus to join our planets by the bye,
sans starship, through the portals in our mind.

Gliese 581d, a rocky sphere,
with thirty days or so to fill a month?
581f? Further … hardly near.
667Cc? Light years? Dear,
t'is twenty-two and in Scorpio spins,
twenty-eight days to a month, and its size
four-times-plus-half our earth—just imagine…
Kepler 22b, we're nearly twins
with climes of 72; my passion
for this planet dares continue to rise.

HD 85512b, 'tis three-
plus-point-six times our earth and with such gales,
a mere thirty-five light years, then we're free!
Cast off—Unfurl those massive solar sails!
Or perhaps we'll journey to the frigid
surface of Gliese 581d, where
to enjoy seven times the space of earth.
'Tis possible our lives might be rigid,
unless some greenhouse gases
flourish there.
Let us join together, find a new berth!

I near forgot Gliese581c,
where light and heat, perhaps, are quite stable.
But let us pause to reflect on SETI,
to ask if communiqués are able
to reach us from these distances so vast.
Will our alien friends prefer to meet
us on their soil or ours, an orbital
station? Or do they watch us quite aghast,
concealed from radar just beyond our keep,
their systems on alert, nondigital?

Arctic oscillations have us frightened,
so much of earth is suffering from droughts;
our populace is hardly enlightened,
by the increasing radiation routes.
What are we to do? How will we journey
away from these annoying pessimists?
For I'm quite sure even as I stand here,
that we must ignore all these agonists.
Who is to judge this trans-stellar tourney,
when we leave this world … and just disappear?

— Terrie Leigh Relf

Author's Note: This poem was inspired, in part, by Discovery.com article, "Gliese 581D: An Exoplanet Fit for Humans?" at http://news.discovery.com/space/exoplanet-gliese-581d-human-habitation-110516.html

The poem is based on "Ode to a Grecian Urn" by John Keats

The Albermarle Incident

Story by Robert Collins - Illustration by Teresa Tunaley

It was another busy year for Lisa Herbert. She was pleased that, so far, there were no serious problems to resolve. Her time was being spent traveling from planet to planet. Many of the towns on the worlds she had visited had approved the Interstellar Trade Compact that she had helped draft. Her travels involved seeing how the Compact was being implemented, and answering the odd question about how it should be interpreted.

One of those worlds was Wright. The town closest to its hyperspace platform was Greensboro. When Lisa arrived there on a typical mid-spring day, she believed the visit wouldn't amount to much. She was so certain that she told her friends and bodyguards, Davis Williams and Josie, to wait at the platform.

Lisa was almost to the mayor's office when a man stopped her on the street. "Are you Lisa Herbert?" he asked.

"Yes." She eased her left hand towards the knife at her hip. She turned back to the platform. Davis and Josie had seen the man heading towards her, for they were jogging in her direction.

The man smiled. "Good. I've been waiting for a couple days. The boredom was starting to get to me."

"Who are you?"

"Oh, sorry. My name's Frank Harris." He stuck out his right hand. Lisa didn't accept it. He noticed an instant later, and dropped his arm. "You've heard of me, then."

"No, I haven't."

"Oh. Well, would you be willing to give me a few minutes of your time?"

Lisa looked over the man. It was a way for her to allow Josie and Davis to reach her. Harris was about average in his height and weight, with dark hair and brown eyes. He was dressed in a white shirt, dark pants, and leather boots. He had a ring on his right ring finger that appeared to be gold, and one on his left that had a tiny red gem sticking out of it. His clothes were clean.

"To do what?" she asked him as her friends arrived.

"To talk." He pointed to an inn a short distance away. "I have a room there. We can take a table in the restaurant. It's quiet right about now."

"You won't mind if my friends come with me?"

"Not at all."

She followed Harris to the inn, with Davis and Josie right behind her. He led them inside and to a table to one side of the restaurant. A young woman came up to them after they sat down and asked what they wanted to drink. Harris asked for a beer; Lisa and her friends chose tea.

"What did you want to talk to me about?" Lisa asked Harris.

"I run a bar in Albermarle. Or, at least I did up until a week ago. Under the new Compact, we chose to hold an election for mayor early. One of the other bar owners, Rich Webster, ran against Mayor Masters, promising to close the bars and clean up the town."

"A bar owner promised that?" Davis asked.

"Yes. You are?"

"This is Davis, and that's Josie," Lisa answered. "Go on."

"He told the two churches in town that he planned to live an honest life if he was elected. Now, we're a port town, like Half Moon Bay, so it can get a little rough every now and again." At that moment the girl returned with their drinks. Harris took that chance to look Lisa in the eyes. "None of us are like that bastard you nailed up there a few years back."

"I'm glad to hear that. And I'm glad to hear that you know what I did. Go on."

"Anyway, Ed—Mayor Masters—didn't think anything of Rich. He didn't think anyone would believe him. I didn't either. As the days got closer, Rich kept at his claim that he was a changed man and was going to clean up the town. Come election day, Rich becomes mayor."

"Was his first act to shut your bar down?"

"Yep."

"What do you want me to do?"

"I'm not finished, Miss Herbert."

"I'm sorry. Continue."

"See, the problem isn't that he's closed my bar. It's that he hasn't closed his."

Lisa took a long drink of her tea before speaking. "That is odd, Mister Harris. Are yours and his the only bars in town?"

"There's two others."

"What's happened to them?"

"Nothing as yet. Rich has said that the first hint of trouble, he'll shut them down. But he hasn't said anything about his bar."

Lisa took another drink, using the time to compose her thoughts. "It could be, Mister Harris, that your new mayor will keep his promise. Do I think it's fair that he didn't start by closing his bar first?"

"No, it's not fair."

"But for me to get involved in this dispute, something more has to happen. I can understand why you're upset, Mister Harris. Things in your town have changed, and you've lost your business because of that change. Right now, though, that's all this is. Change. If, in three months, or six months, or whenever, the new mayor still has his bar open, and he's closed the other two, then that's a problem."

Harris was quiet for a moment, drinking his beer. Finally he said, "I guess I see your point, Miss Herbert. But, down the road, if his place is still open, and he's closed the others, would you be willing to help me out?"

"Yes. That's a problem I'd be willing to help resolve."

"Fair enough. I'll head back home tomorrow. Thanks for talking to me, Miss Herbert."

"Sure. Thank you for the tea. I hope everything works out for you, Mister Harris."

* * *

When Lisa, Davis, and Josie returned to Wright, Lisa didn't tell them to wait. The memory of Harris approaching her some weeks back was fresh in her mind. She let them follow her from the hyperspace platform to Greensboro.

Once again, before she could reach the mayor's office, Harris met her on the street. "Miss Herbert, we need to talk."

She was about to tell him to wait when she looked at his face. The part of his face around his left eye had the markings of a bruise. It wasn't a black eye, but it was clear he'd had one recently.

"What happened to you?"

"Let's get out of the heat and talk."

"Sure."

She followed him to the same inn where they had spoken on her last visit. He led them to a table in the restaurant, but this time when the girl asked what they would have, Harris ordered two beers.

"I went back home, like I said I would," Harris said. "Things were quiet for a week or so. Then Rich closed down the other two bars. Here's the thing: he closed them because a man came out of one and threw up in the street."

"That's bad," Davis said, "but hardly a crime."

Harris nodded. "That's the excuse Rich used to shut them down. That's not the half of it. He had the other two owners arrested and charged with disrupting the peace."

"Were they convicted?" Lisa asked.

"There hasn't been a trial yet. I went to Rich and asked when they'd be tried. He said it was none of my business. That night a couple guys came to my house. They rushed me. One of them held me while his friend gave me a black eye and a few licks to the belly. After the other guy let me go, his friend said that if I didn't leave town in the morning, they'd be back the next night. I left, and for the past week and a day I've been staying here."

Lisa leaned forward. "All you did was ask when the other two men would be tried? You didn't get angry, make any threats, nothing like that?"

"Hell, I just asked. When Rich said to butt out, the only thing I said was that I was just asking, to be fair."

"That's all?"

"I thought I'd caught him on a bad day. The only other thing I said was, as I left, that I'd ask again at a better time. I swear, Miss Herbert, I didn't do anything to provoke him."

"That sounds bad."

"So you're going to help?"

"What about the other people in town? How do they feel?"

"Once those two bars closed, there were lots of folks mad, but quite a few were happy to see them gone. Town's divided, Miss Herbert, in a way I've never seen before."

Lisa shook her head. "That's not good, Mister Harris. On the one hand, it certainly sounds like your new mayor isn't a good person. On the other hand, it sounds like he has some support for what he's doing. I tell you what. I'll mention this to Mayor Roberts and get his view. I'll talk to a few other mayors about it on my way back home. If they think I should do something, I'll come right back. Otherwise, you may need to wait another month or so."

Harris frowned. "I hope you'll come right back, but I guess if you don't want to deal with a divided town, then I guess I can't blame you."

"One way or the other, I'll keep in touch with you."

"Thanks."

Lisa rose, followed by her friends. She led them straight from the inn to the Greensboro town hall. She had to wait a while for Mayor Roberts to end his meeting. Once it was over he welcomed her into his office.

"Did you speak to Harris?" the Mayor asked before Lisa could sit down.

"I did." She glanced at Davis and Josie. They nodded. "My friends and I would like to believe his story. Is it true?"

"I think so. He's not the only one who was asked to leave."

"Who else was told to leave?"

"One of the fishermen. I only know about the man because he got really drunk here once. I think two or three other men have been forced to leave Albermarle," Davis said.

"Sounds like just the big drinkers," Davis said.

"Except that fisherman is a nice guy when he's sober. When we arrested him, he apologized the next day. Said something like, once he got into a glass, it was hard for him to get out. Anyway, a week later a box of fish filets came here. There was a note from the man, apologizing again and hoping the fish would pay for the trouble he'd caused."

Lisa nodded. "That was nice of him."

"Yeah. The others, they're just drunks. But tossing the fisherman out of town?" The mayor shook his head. "Doesn't sound right to me, Miss Herbert."

"Do you hear anything else from people there about what's going on, Mayor?"

"Some of the folks who come down here to trade say it's fine, and some say it's unfair. From what Harris told me, sounds like Albermarle is split down the middle."

"Keep watch on the situation, Mayor. Send word to me if it gets worse. I'm going to talk to a few other mayors on other worlds and get their views. I don't want to do anything if the town's divided."

* * *

Lisa let out a long breath. "So, that's what's going. Any thoughts?"

Her father took a bite of dinner, ate it, then shook his head. "This Webster sounds like a man up to no good. Have you considered going there yourself?"

"I did, but I'm not sure it's a good idea."

"Why not?"

"It seems to me that this mayor can't be acting on his own. I know that on Wright town laws are enforced by a sheriff. Webster has to have the town sheriff on his side."

"That makes sense."

"That's two men. How can two men stand up to several? Webster has to have a group helping him."

"Again, makes sense."

"If that's the case, then even if I go with Davis and Josie, we'd be outnumbered. We could get tossed in jail if Webster doesn't like what I have to say."

Her father nodded. "Yes, I see. As long as Webster has the support of other people in town, aside from any men working for him, you can't force him out."

"No." Lisa took a couple of bites of dinner before speaking again. "Webster seems to be one of those

men who wants power. Those men always go too far. I think if I wait, I'll be better able to deal with him."

"There's something else, Lisa."

"What?"

"It also sounds like Webster wants to get his way, no matter what. He wants to run the town. He wants to have the only bar, so he wants all that business."

"That's right. Men who always want to get their way don't like people disagreeing with them. I guess that means sooner or later he's going to force someone out of town who's more popular than those bar owners." She nodded. "That's the time to act."

"That time may come sooner than you think. You'd better be ready for it, Lisa."

* * *

Lisa was back on Wright almost two months after her second visit. Like on the previous visit, Davis and Josie were with her. As she entered the town of Greensboro she was once again met by Frank Harris.

"Are things worse?" she asked him.

"Yep. This time, though, the mayor wants to join us."

"I'll go get him. Are you still at that inn?"

"Yes, and I'm not the only one."

That's not good, Lisa thought. "Gather whoever you need to. We'll be right there."

Harris nodded and went back to the inn. Lisa headed to the town hall. This time the mayor cut off his meeting. "Are you going to talk to Harris and the others?"

"Yes. He said you wanted to be there."

"I do."

The mayor followed her, Davis, and Josie to the inn. Inside the restaurant three tables were being shoved together by two men. Once the tables were together chairs were laid out around them. Harris asked Lisa to sit at one end of the group. Davis and Josie took seats to the right and left of her. Harris sat down next to Davis on Lisa's right, the mayor next to Josie on her left.

Harris introduced the other three men who were joining them. Two were the other bar owners, Luke Brown and Bill Dane. The third was the Reverend Neal Pettis, pastor of the town's Baptist Church.

"Why are you here, Reverend?" Lisa asked.

"I was forced out like these three," he replied. "About four weeks ago I gave a sermon at which I said it was wrong for Mayor Webster to keep his bar open when he had promised to clean up the town. Two days later he came to see me. He said that I shouldn't criticize how he was doing his job. I told him that he wasn't doing all he'd promised.

"The following Sunday I gave another sermon. One of the 'patrons' of his bar was in the church that day. After the sermon I told the congregation that the mayor had expressed his unhappiness with the previous week's sermon. I said that I had expressed my disappointment in him. I said to the congregation that if they were also disappointed, to speak to Mayor Webster.

"That night his men came to my house and dragged me to jail. The next morning Webster said that I could be charged with disturbing the peace, or that I could leave town. I refused to leave. He charged me, staged a trial that night with his men as jurors, and they convicted me. I spent a week in jail. At the end of the week Webster said I could leave, or get charged again. I didn't need to be told twice."

Lisa glanced around at the others for a moment. "I take it there's another church in town? What about their minister?"

"Will Barclay has the Methodist congregation. He's getting up in years, Miss Herbert. A friend has come here since then, telling me that he's going to keep quiet. I don't blame him; a stay in jail might ruin his health."

"Do the people still support Mayor Webster?"

"Not at all."

"Why don't they do something?" Josie asked.

"Young lady, they're craftsmen and fishermen. Webster's friends have been in a few brawls over their lives. They have clubs and crossbows. If the people tried to start something, several of them would get hurt, or worse."

"It's not just that," Harris added. "Most folks have to work six days a week to have enough to eat, to have good clothes and blankets, and to take care of everything else. To do something would take time, time that these folks just can't spare."

Lisa turned to the mayor of Greensboro. "Have you talked to the other mayors on this world about this?"

He nodded. "We want to see Webster go, but we don't have the means, either. I've been asked to request your aid. If you'll help us, I'd be happy to put Webster and his friends on trial here. This situation has everyone upset."

"There's at least a dozen people here who left or were forced out," Harris said. "They'd be happy to help you, Miss Herbert."

"Do any of them know how to fight?"

"Not really."

"Then I won't need them." Lisa turned to Davis. "I told Ned not to stray too far from the portals. Find him, and tell him to bring everyone here as fast as they can." *Sometimes it's good that your business partner is a reformed outlaw,* she mused.

She turned to the others. "Josie and I will head back to my home to get our weapons. We'll be back here by nightfall. I want you and your friends here to wait. My friends are experienced at fighting, moving at night, and so on. We'll deal with Webster and his gang."

"You're not going to kill them?" Pettis asked.

"Not unless we have no other choice." She smiled. "Don't worry. I think we can end this trouble without anyone getting hurt." She let her smile fade. "That doesn't mean I'm going to ask him nicely to stop."

* * *

Lisa knew that she and her friends couldn't ride their own mounts to Ablermarle. They'd be heard, even if they stopped a mile or so from town. With the help of the mayor of Greensboro, she was able to borrow a wagon. That meant it would take three-quarters of a day to reach Albermarle.

She decided to make it an all-day trip. She knew she was out of practice at both sneaking around and fighting; she guessed that the others could use some practice as well. Every so often they would pause work out, fire off a few shots, and otherwise prepare for their arrival.

She knew from her visits to Wright that first they had to get through the town of Wilsonton. It sat along a small creek. From Greensboro to Wilsonton the land was wooded and slightly hilly. Wilsonton marked the point where the landscape changed to that of a flatter plain near the coast.

The town itself was small, half the size of Albermarle and a third the size of Greensboro. The mayor there was happy to see Lisa, and happy to know what she was up to. "A few folks here have relations in Albermarle," he said. "They're worried about them."

"Anyone that's a friend of Mayor Webster?" Lisa asked.

"Not at all."

"All the same, I don't want anyone going to Albermarle once we leave. It'll be easier for everyone if our arrival is a surprise."

"I'll keep a lid on this, sure."

Satisfied, Lisa rejoined her friends and they had an early lunch. They continued on, pausing a few more times along the way. Lisa recalled that while the land near the coast was flat, the road would pass over a good-sized hill two miles from Albermarle. Lisa decided that would be the place where the group would make camp. They ate an early dinner, then rested.

Lisa assigned watch duty to Night Hawk. He was the brother of one of her first off-world friends, Little Wolf. They lived in a "tribe" on White Rocks. Two years ago the tribe had moved to a world that Lisa found had been depopulated by the Savage Rain. It was during that time that she met Night Hawk. The young man admired her, and was eager to join her.

She put his skills to use scouting a world that had come to exist on raiding their neighboring planets. When it was time to stop those raids, Night Hawk scouted for Lisa's little army. Because of that, she knew that he'd be able to reach Albermarle quietly, and return to their camp without endangering the group.

Before heading out she talked to the folks who had left Albermarle. They had told her that on weeknights Webster closed his bar early at around ten. The sheriff would walk the town after that, then go to the jail to spend the night. Webster's other henchmen would spend the night at his bar. She told Night Hawk to watch for when Webster closed the bar; that would be their time to move.

Several hours after she had fallen asleep she was awakened. She looked up; Night Hawk was shaking her. "Is it time?" she asked in a low voice.

"The lights in the building you told me to watch have gone out," he said. "Two men just left the building."

"Good. Wake the others."

She rose and stretched. She checked to make sure she still had one knife sheathed at her hip and another in her right boot. She picked up her crossbow and slung it over her shoulder.

Once the others were awake she patted Night Hawk's shoulder. "Get some rest. I won't send for you till morning."

He nodded. "Be safe, Lisa."

She nodded back. She turned to Davis. "Let's go."

Her group marched slowly in single file down one side of the road. The planet's moon was half-bright. That was good; when it was a full moon it was bright enough to let someone see quite a ways away. All the same they moved with care and caution. At the edge of town they left the road, went around a building, and headed into the alley between those on the main road and those on one of the three parallel streets.

Lisa had debated with herself about the best way to deal with the sheriff. The best option was to catch him while he was still making his rounds. However, creeping across two miles of road, then walking a block and a half would take time. If he was still around when they got close to the jail, they'd act. If not, Lisa prepared for her backup plan.

As it was, they reached the back of the jail after the sheriff had finished his rounds. The small wooden building had a back door as well as a front door. The back door had a window but no shade on the other side. Seeing that, Lisa took off her crossbow and handed it to Josie. Lisa had put her hair into a pony tail; she untied it and let her hair fall around her shoulders.

She pointed to Ned. He wasn't as muscular as Davis, but he was much quicker. She indicated a spot next to the door. He nodded and loaded his crossbow. She walked up to the back door and waited for him.

Once he was ready, she banged on the door. "Help!" she said in a slightly raised voice. She kept pounding the door. "Sheriff! Help! Help me!"

A light came on from inside. A man with brown hair and a scar on his left cheek peeked out the window. He had a lantern in his hand.

Lisa glanced left then cried, "Help me! Let me in!"

She heard a metallic sound. The door opened a crack. "Who are you, Miss?" the man asked.

Lisa jerked the door open. "You have to help me!" She grabbed the man's free hand and used it to pull herself inside. She kept hold of it and turned him around.

"What? Why?"

Ned came through an instant later. Lisa could tell from the sheriff's panicked expression that Ned had pushed the business end of his crossbow into the man's back.

"I'm Lisa Herbert," she whispered. "Do as you're told and you won't get hurt."

"Sure," the sheriff replied.

She walked past three empty jail cells to the room that was the sheriff's office. Ned prodded the sheriff behind her. The rest of her group entered the building.

Lisa took the lantern from the sheriff and placed it on his desk. "How many men are at the bar, Sheriff?"

"Seven."

"Do you and Mayor Webster have any more men working for you?"

"What do you mean?"

"Answer her," Ned snapped.

The sheriff jerked forward. "No! Those are all the guys we got!"

"Is the mayor at home?" Lisa asked.

"Yeah."

"Does he still come to his bar for breakfast every morning?"

"Yeah, sure."

"Good. Let's go to Webster's bar. You're going to help us wake the men up."

"Me?"

"Yes, you. If you don't want to get hurt, you won't say or do anything that makes this harder for us."

The man nodded. His eyes darted around.

"Do you have the keys to the bar?"

"Uh, no."

"Why were you looking around, then?" She glanced at Davis. "Check the desk."

Davis started opening drawers. The second opened with the sound of metal clinking together. He took out three rings with a dozen keys on each one.

"Most lawmen are given keys to the local businesses," Lisa said. "They're supposed to be used to get into them in case of fire or some other problem. I hope you and Webster haven't been abusing this duty, Sheriff. Which one is the right one?"

Davis showed the rings to the sheriff. The sheriff picked the middle one. He held the ring up when he came to the fourth key.

"Good." Lisa went to the front door, unlocked it, and opened it. "Lead the way."

The sheriff walked out with Ned still close at his back. Lisa's four other guards followed Ned. Lisa nodded to Davis. He nodded back, and he and Josie headed for the back door. Lisa went through the front door and closed it quietly.

The group walked for half a block to Webster's bar. There were two big windows to either side of the front door. Shades had been pulled down behind them, as had one on the window of the door. The word "Closed" was painted on the door window shade.

Lisa passed by her group to stand behind Ned. Ned jabbed his crossbow into the sheriff's back. The sheriff put the key into a box next to the door. There was a hiss, and the door swung back into the building. Ned shoved the sheriff inside. Lisa rushed behind him and held the door. The other four followed her in.

She caught sight of seven men sleeping on the floor of the bar. Tables and chairs had been stacked to one side. The commotion woke the men up. While she bent down to guard the sheriff, Ned and the rest pointed their crossbows at the men. Two of the men had been sleeping towards the back, where the drinks were mixed and served. They rose and ran for the back

door. Lisa heard the door open, followed by a skidding noise. A moment later they returned, with Davis and Josie watching them with loaded crossbows.

Lisa waited for her friends to get all of Webster's henchmen, including the sheriff, lined up and facing her. When that was done she said simply, "Hello, I'm Lisa Herbert, and you men are in a lot of trouble."

She turned to Ned. "Tie them up."

"All right, you," Ned said to the men, "turn around."

Aside from the wagon, Lisa had also secured a few lengths of thin rope before leaving Greensboro. She had Ned and two others carry the lengths with them. Ned took his from his right hip as had been agreed. He approached the sheriff first. He pulled the man's hands behind his back and tied his wrists together. Ned took the rest of his rope and tied up two more men. He used a second length to tie up three more, and the third to bind the last two.

While Ned was tying up the rest, Davis and Josie forced the first three men to lie on the floor face-down. They did the same with the second trio and the final pair of men. Lisa instructed Davis and Josie to take the first watch. She and the rest of her group sat down in chairs and tried to sleep.

I may not get comfortable, she assured herself wryly, *but at least my hands aren't tied behind my back.*

Lisa slept through the night. Her neck felt stiff when she was awakened at dawn, but some stretching eased the discomfort. While Ned and another young man woke up the others, Lisa searched the bar for food. She found eggs and bacon. She got a fire going in the stove and started cooking.

She had Davis go to the entrance of the bar. He would look through the side of one window shade, walk to the other side of the shade and look out, walk to the other shade, look out of both sides of it, then go back. He went through that routine several times.

Lisa had finished breakfast for half of her friends when Davis stopped and turned to her. "He's coming," he announced.

"You guys know what to do," Lisa said.

Ned and two of her guards were already sitting at a table. They drew their knives and put them on the table in front of them. Josie and the other two were at another table. They picked up their crossbows and loaded them. Davis picked up and loaded his crossbow, then moved to a spot next to the door that would allow him to point his weapon at the back of anyone who came in.

A quiet moment passed and the door opened.

Lisa watched as a woman about her age came through the door, followed by a man about a decade older. The woman was fair-haired, short, and buxom. The man was of average height and weight, had dark hair and brown eyes, and had a thin mustache. The woman's dress was frilly; the man's clothes clean but otherwise ordinary.

"Come in, Mayor," Lisa called. She turned to the woman. "You must be the mayor's wife. Come in!"

"Who are you?" Webster asked. Davis, without a prompt from Lisa, stuck the business end of his crossbow into Webster's back. Webster let out a gasp. "What's going on?"

"I'm Lisa Herbert. I've heard some very bad things about you, Mayor."

"What do you mean?"

"Oh, come on. You lied to get people's votes. You've closed down your rivals. You've forced people out of town simply for challenging you."

"My Rich is a strong man!" Webster's wife shouted back. "Strong men hang on to what they have! You can't come here and stop that!"

"Your husband has broken laws," Lisa replied calmly.

"He didn't break any laws!"

"I think he's broken just about every clause in the Interstellar Compact."

"I didn't sign it," Webster said.

"That doesn't matter. The previous mayor did, with the support of the people here. That makes it binding. If we disobeyed laws because we didn't have anything to do with drafting them, there wouldn't be any laws."

"You've got no right to interfere," Webster's wife insisted.

"For Mother's sake," Josie snapped. She put her crossbow on the table, stood up, walked to Webster's wife, and slapped her in the face.

"Josie!" Lisa called.

"I'm sorry, Lisa, but I couldn't listen to this crap any longer." She turned to Webster's wife. "Being a leader means being better than the people you lead."

"He is better!"

Josie slapped her again. "No, he isn't! Someone better leads by example. Thinks of others first. Treats others the way they want to be treated. Men like your husband caused the Savage Rain. Women like you who stand up for them make it worse for the rest of us."

"I'd shut up if I were you," Davis said. "Josie here could take you down with one hand tied behind her back."

The room was quiet for a moment. At last Ned said, "I hope you're not burning breakfast, Lisa. I'm really hungry."

"No, it's fine." She turned to the Websters. "You'll face serious punishment soon enough. First, though, you'll have to sit and watch us eat."

A Taste of
Copper

Story by Lance J. Mushung
Illustration by Neil T. Foster

They arrived on a Tuesday morning. I was at work at Jack Engineering, JE to the employees, when my phone chirped. "Hammond, good morning," I said into the handset.

"Andy, check the news," my buddy Scott's breathless voice told me, and then he hung up.

The Internet news showed a massive object, it had to be a spaceship, hanging over the U.N. building in New York. It looked like a smooth copper egg and was at least 2000 feet long, judging from the buildings it floated over. The color reminded me of the Coppertone kitchen appliances that had been popular when I was a kid.

About a dozen people, Scott included, were in the conference room with the big TV when I got there. The TV showed the ship while the news anchors talked and talked, making inane comments that demonstrated they didn't know anything. Most of my coworkers looked frightened, but Martin had a smug grin as if some great conspiracy had been confirmed. He was one of the people who believed aliens landed on the roof of the building every night and had a right to be smug. He'd been more correct than all the people who'd pooh-poohed the very concept of alien visitors, including myself. For most of my 57 years I'd read science fiction, but even after all that I'd never expected to see aliens.

Sci-fi almost always said aliens were hostile. What would I do if they were? I could go to the small ranch I'd bought as a retirement home. But it was awfully close to the city if the aliens were indeed hostile. Could I become a survivalist? Regular exercise meant I was still in pretty decent shape. But the sun burning my pale skin and giving my hazel eyes cataracts weren't very appealing thoughts. And then there were the joys of living off the land, sleeping under the stars with bugs chewing on me, and squatting in the bush until some illness finished me off. I might have been able to pull it off 20 years earlier, but not any longer.

The TV caught my attention when the news anchors, looking shaken, said Chicago had been destroyed. A chill ran up and down my spine. These aliens hadn't come for a benign visit.

Reports of more devastated cities came in and everyone but Martin and me ran out of the room. They must have been worried we'd be a target too, but I reasoned we'd already have been dead if the aliens had wanted that. After 30 minutes the news reports agreed that eleven cities had been obliterated. Chicago, Mexico City, Buenos Aires, Jakarta, Beijing, Shanghai, New Delhi, Mumbai, Cairo, Lagos, and Moscow were all gone.

The cameras zoomed in on one end of the ship. A small craft, it looked like a tiny version of the mother ship, had exited through a hatch that appeared and disappeared as if by magic. The craft, a shuttle it seemed, descended to First Avenue where the U. N. Secretary General was standing in front of a microphone about 100 yards from anyone else.

"Look at the Secretary General," I said to Martin. "He's one hell of a tool, but you've got to give him points for guts."

The shuttle came to rest 30 feet from the Secretary General and floated without a sound a few feet off the pavement. A hatch appeared, a ramp extended, and two space suits colored like shiny pennies appeared. They were perhaps four-feet tall and had two arms and two legs. The helmets were mirrored, concealing the heads of whatever was inside, and unlike human suits there were no backpacks, tubes or panels evident.

"I wonder what's with the suits?" Martin said.

"I guess our air is bad for them. Or maybe they're afraid of germs. Could it be something as simple as the temperature being too high or low?"

"What if the aliens aren't in the suits at all? Maybe they're robots."

The suits stopped within a yard of the Secretary General and he said, "I greet you in the name of all humans and respectfully request—"

"We are the Scarn," a deep voice interrupted. "You are now chattel of our domain. We find it useful to give an object lesson when we encounter a new planet. You are now certain that we are serious, are you not?"

"We all believe you're serious. May I ask why you've come?"

"To add your chattel to our domain as we just stated. All of you now serve us. We, at first, require 11% of your world's output as tribute. After you organize to better serve us, that will rise by a factor of three. Details will be communicated over the next few days, along with our regulations. Any resistance will be dealt with harshly. We are done for now."

The aliens turned and re-boarded their shuttle. The Secretary General must have been taken aback. His jaw moved, but no words came out.

"I hope chattel was an unfortunate translation," Martin said.

My facial expression said I thought he must be kidding.

There was no doubt my career with defense

contractors was over, and moving to my ranch seemed the best bet. I called my good friends Barry and Carla Campbell to let them know I was coming. I'd worked with Barry for many years before he and Carla had bought their ranch, and I bought the place next to theirs when I saw the beauty of the area. In return for watching over my property, they used my barn and grazed their animals on my pastures.

I left a resignation letter in JE's vacant HR department. Quitting didn't bother me. My first JE boss, after a contract change had forced me to work for the company, was English and forthright. He'd told me JE was rubbish, and he'd known what he was talking about. Fingering out, quitting while giving JE a middle finger, had been one of my favorite fantasies for some time.

We soon learned the Scarn wanted their tribute in the form of raw and refined materials, specialty chemicals, and a wide range of manufactured goods. It was hard to believe they couldn't produce the items themselves with less trouble than invading us. On the other hand, why do things yourself when you could force someone else to do them for free?

They seemed to have a burning lust for copper and made a special point of demanding it. Even pennies were pulled out of circulation, although it had been decades since they'd contained much copper. I recalled a movie in which aliens used copper to run their technology and thought perhaps that was it.

The Scarn did encounter a setback seen by the world at a ceremonial surrender of the army at Fort Benning. Two Scarn met a four-star army general and a few of his staff on a viewing stand. The general looked like a Hollywood stereotype with his chiseled jaw, gray short hair, and ramrod straight posture. When the space suits were before him he said, "I do this for all mankind." A second later the viewing stand was replaced by the dust and smoke of a massive explosion. The TV went blank, but later showed the Scarn's retribution for the army's tiny success. A strike from orbit had made Fort Benning a collection of smoking craters. It was heartening to know the Scarn weren't bombproof, but the price for that bit of information had been high.

Nothing that even hinted at problems was ever reported by the media again. The Internet became the source of occasional accounts, more like whispers, of actions against the Scarn and their agents. It was fortunate industry had come to rely on the Internet so much. The Scarn couldn't just turn it off.

It seemed Scarn policies were implemented overnight. Environmental regulations were abolished if they conflicted with the production of anything the Scarn wanted. All governments began looking at anyone over 55 to ensure the seniors were still productive. Old folks in poor health were simply denied medication and treatment. Murdering them outright would be next, I figured. But one of the policies wasn't so bad and put a wry grin on my face whenever I thought of it. Most lawyers had been banned after the Scarn stated attorneys were detrimental to productivity.

The Scarn wanted humans to take care of day-to-day affairs and they made deals with the lowest types of humans, the ones for whom having power meant all. Cartels, street gangs, and biker gangs were the types selected and put above human law, provided they enforced Scarn policies. They ensured the unimpeded production of items the Scarn wanted and took care of anti-Scarn activities, along with their usual shady pursuits. I was disgusted by how they'd sold out, had become traitors to their species.

The enforcers in my area were bikers who liked calling themselves a motorcycle club. They were the greasy-looking cockroaches TV had taught me to expect. I'd never seen more dark jeans, black leather, unkempt beards, do-rags, and inked skin in one place.

The bikers started off nasty, and became overbearing and arrogant in no time as power went to their heads. I ignored them and their outrages and spent my time helping Barry and Carla with ranch chores. But one day changed everything. After a shopping trip to town, I came home and found an ambulance at Barry and Carla's place. My car skidded to a stop next to a paramedic and I jumped out saying, "What's going on?"

"The couple who own this ranch were shot dead. We're taking them to the morgue."

The world began spinning and I was close to throwing up, but I managed to choke out, "Where's the goddamn sheriff."

"He's come and gone. Are you all right?"

I didn't answer and got back in my car. Sheriff Butler was on the phone when I got to his office. Anyone in Hollywood would have cast him as redneck sheriff. He had a bit of a beer belly, a round tanned face, and thinning blond hair. I didn't listen to his phone conversation, but did notice his distinctive Texas drawl. He motioned me to sit down in front of his desk as he put down the handset.

"I'm Andy Hammond, a close friend of the Campbells from the ranch next door. What the hell happened?"

"Our bikers were sport-shooting animals from the road. Your friends objected and were shot dead for their trouble."

"What are you going to do about it?"

"Nothing."

"What do you mean nothing? There's got to be something?"

He shook his head. "I'm mighty sorry, but there's not. Not under the present system. The bikers get a pass on everything."

"Nobody can do anything?"

"Not even the FBI could touch them. It's been turned into the Friggin' Bureau of Impotence anyway. I'm not a fan of coarse language, but you can guess what the F really stands for. Then again, some thought it was that before the Scarn."

"I'm executer of their wills. Can I proceed on their affairs?"

"You can. The matter of their deaths is closed."

I arranged funerals for the following afternoon. There was no reason to delay. Nobody could travel from out of town to attend. My last arrangements of the day were for neighbors to help me care for Barry and Carla's animals from then on.

That evening it hit me. My friends were gone and tears streaked my cheeks. Maybe they'd be alive if anybody had stood up to the bikers in the beginning. If only I'd done something to resist the turds. It took little time for rage to replace sorrow, and I knew any justice would have to come from me. "I'll have to kill the bastards myself," I mumbled out loud.

Should I do it, could I do it? I'd never killed anything larger than an insect before. Target shooting had been my game. But going over and over all the things the bikers had done convinced me that they were less than insects. Even so, I wrestled with the idea of killing them for hours. I told myself again and again that they were toilet film, which became my personal mantra.

Would I get myself killed? The smart money said yes. Even if the bikers didn't kill me, someone else coming to the ranch afterwards to get me would. But the thought of death no longer bothered me much. I was already over 55, a dangerous age with the Scarn in charge. I didn't relish the idea of being euthanized while strapped down on a gurney or deteriorating one agonizing day after another because I couldn't get some medication or treatment. And besides, I'd never wanted to end up like the people I'd seen in rest homes. Drooling into a cup while pissing and pooping into a diaper was about as frightening as it got.

It struck me that some guy plotting to get even was an incredible cliché. Was I that cliché? Did such vengeance ever happen in real life? I remembered the tale of Wyatt Earp avenging his brothers and felt better that it had at least once.

Deciding where to take on the bikers was easy. Everyone knew they had an all-hands meeting every Tuesday evening in their clubhouse located on the outskirts of town. I saw it every time I went shopping. It was a T-shaped building with the top of the T facing the road. The back was visible from a bend in the road and looked like a row of rooms. A charitable person would have said the rooms were offices. But some of the bikers lived in the clubhouse, so it was obvious the rooms were for sleeping and porking the ho skanks I'd often seen hanging around. I'd have sooner put my dick into a pencil sharpener than one of them.

Across the street from the clubhouse was something I could use, a dilapidated strip center containing only a couple of shops that weren't open at night. I pulled into the center's parking lot the evening after the funeral. The clubhouse had large windows along the front wall and the bikers didn't bother with window coverings. With the lights blazing I could see inside with no trouble. The front was a rec area and bar. The left wall had a sliding glass door, and a pool table covered by red felt was close by. A few stuffed chairs in a tan-orange color were scattered here and there. To the right, behind the front door, restaurant-style tables and chairs were arranged in front of the bar made of dark wood. On the back wall near the bar, I spotted the entryway of the hall going to the back rooms. The building wasn't fortified. Why would it be? The bikers were the top dogs and figured nobody had the guts to take them on in their house.

There were around 15 of the scumbags, and I needed a way to even the odds. A machine gun would have been great, but I didn't know how to get one. Making a simple one, like the Stens the British churned out during World War II, wasn't supposed to be all that difficult. But I didn't have the right machining skills. Making a semi-automatic into an automatic was possible, but again I didn't have the skills.

Explosives were attractive. My knowledge was once again not up to the job though. I didn't know how to make them out of household chemicals, and increasing my knowledge wasn't going to happen. The Scarn had put spiders to work trolling the Internet to destroy information on weapons. I was aware of ANFO, ammonium nitrate and fuel oil, but recalled it needed an energetic detonator, which was something

I didn't have. Asking for blasting caps or primer cord around town wasn't much of an idea.

I'd made a steeple out of my fingers and was stroking my lip when an idea came to me like the proverbial bolt from the blue. A pickup filled with gas would be something like an explosive. It wouldn't actually blow up, but would produce one hell of a fire.

I'd need a way to ignite the gas. A fuse didn't seem very practical. A flare gun would work, but what if I missed? Remembering war movies gave me the solution, a Molotov cocktail. I'd put a load of gasoline in an open container near the tailgate and an open flame, like a propane torch, at the front of the bed. The gas would slosh forward when the truck hit the clubhouse and turn into a fireball. Some sort of flimsy barrier between the gas and the open flame would take care of igniting any vapors early, but wouldn't prevent the gas from sloshing forward.

The hobby Barry and I dabbled in so many years before gave me a way to get the truck to the clubhouse. We'd played with RC controlled model boats and planes, and some of the boats used pretty big actuators. Barry still had the gear in his garage.

After setting the right side of the clubhouse ablaze by crashing the truck through the front door, I could go in the sliding glass door and finish the bikers with gunfire. Afterwards I had all night to hoof it back home if I wasn't dead.

I slept little that night, and dawn saw me in Barry's garage tracking down actuators and a controller. I didn't need much, just enough for control of the pedals and some basic steering.

I bolted a bar onto the floorboard of Barry's rusty old blue F-150 right in front of the driver's seat and attached actuators to stomp on the pedals. Then I mounted a push-pull actuator with a rod going to the left side of the steering wheel. It would turn the wheel about 20 degrees each way, which was more than enough. And I could still drive the truck with the pedal actuators turned off and the rod disconnected from the steering wheel. What I had wouldn't let me remotely drive it across the state, or even across town for that matter. But it would let me send it on its way straight across the street from the strip center to the clubhouse.

Like all real ranchers, Barry had a ton of stuff in his barn and garage. I found pans, gas cans, and torches in no time. In a couple of hours the bed was ready. All I'd need to do at the strip center was pour gas into the pans and light the torch.

I got my 1911A1 .45 ACP, 12-gauge riot pump, ammo, holster, and other gear out of their hiding place. I slid eight 00-buckshot shells into the shotgun's tube magazine and set aside another 22 shells. An evil little laugh escaped my lips when I picked up a copper jacketed .45 round. The biker scum would soon get to taste something the Scarn always want, copper. I loaded five seven-round magazines and put one into the pistol. The pistol's heft felt reassuring. It might be more than 100-year-old technology, but it could still take care of business. I put the weapons behind the seat under a blanket.

I repeated my toilet film mantra a number of times the next day, Tuesday. In the fading light of a clear and cool evening, I drove to the strip center and parked in the lot with the truck aimed at the clubhouse's front door. The number of motorcycles said the bikers were all there. There weren't any street or parking lot lights, but the half-moon shining down provided enough illumination for my work. In around ten minutes my firebomb pickup was ready.

I clipped the pistol holster onto my belt and nodded my head about the satisfying metallic snickering sound of the pistol's slide as I chambered a round. After lowering the hammer, I shoved the gun into the holster. I rested my shotgun on a parking block and put the extra magazines and shotgun shells into the pockets of my windbreaker.

My heart was pounding and sweat moistened my palms. The stars were a magnificent sight, and I gazed up at them for a few moments. It was a crime such beauty held things like the Scarn.

I exhaled a breath as if every molecule leaving my lungs was precious. A glance both ways down the street confirmed there was no traffic, as I'd expected. I reached through the open window and turned the key. The engine came to life and in the quiet of the night rumbled like a caged beast. I slipped the gear selector into drive and using the controller accelerated the truck as if it carried nitroglycerin, which in a way it did. Once in the clubhouse parking lot, I hit the gas and the engine roared. The truck plowed through the clubhouse's front door at something like 35 mph. Along with the jarring sound of the crash, the firebomb ignited with a whoosh and yellow-orange ball of fire.

I dropped the controller, grabbed the shotgun, and jogged to the clubhouse's sliding glass door. Screams of agony split the night for a short time, and I gritted my teeth in response until I began breathing harder from exertion. The glass had popped out of the door and shattered, saving me the trouble of breaking it myself. I took a deep breath and worked the shotgun's pump action. The scary sound steeled my nerves, and I went through the door accompanied by the crunching of my boots on broken glass.

The truck was resting against the bar in the center of an inferno. The room was bright from the dancing yellow flames and the lights that were still on. Splintered tables and shattered chairs, many burning, were strewn about. Seven or eight bikers were on the floor among the debris. At least two were under the truck with their skin already incinerated. The stench of burnt flesh struck my nose and almost gagged me.

Four bikers near me were moving their arms and legs in what looked like slow motion, as if stunned. I yelled something incomprehensible and took no notice of the gun's report and recoil as I pulled the trigger and pumped the action as fast as I could. Buckshot swept the room until there was just a click when I pulled the trigger. The shotgun was empty and no bikers were moving.

Boiling smoke was making it harder to see, but I still spotted movement in the hall running by the back rooms. I dropped the shotgun and drew my .45, thumbing the hammer back as I aimed at the entryway. A fat biker burst out toward me. My gun bucked with a whomping bark twice, and he yelped and crumpled like the proverbial sack of potatoes.

Embers from the fire were falling on the chair I ducked behind, and the fabric was smoldering and becoming black in spots. The incongruous thought that it looked like a leopard jumped to mind.

"I'm going to kill you good, you prick," a biker shouted. He was taking cover by the entryway. "Did you hear me? I'll wipe my ass with your tongue." A gunshot from what sounded like a 12 gauge followed. "I'll get you because I have an edge. I don't give a shit about anything."

"What makes you think I do?" I shouted back in as sarcastic a tone as I could. Responding to taunts from biker trash was useless, but it felt good. I followed up by firing three rounds toward his voice.

After ramming a fresh magazine into my .45, I headed back toward the door and heard the distinctive crunching of someone stepping on broken glass. A couple of seconds later I was looking through my gun's sights at a tall thin biker with a long beard. Running right into me must have been quite a surprise because he froze with wide eyes as if he'd encountered something from Jurassic Park. I fired two rapid shots and he collapsed with blood stains spreading on his chest.

I heard the boom of a 12 gauge and felt an excruciating pain in my left shoulder. It was like the burns I'd gotten as a kid combined with a tooth needing a root canal. I fell to my knees and doubled over with the top of my head on the floor.

"Got you dickhead," the biker yelled. "I told you I would."

The talky lowlife sounded both triumphant and arrogant. He liked trash talk and it was a good bet he watched too much TV too. He'd come over to gloat, and looking between my legs I saw he was. It would be the last mistake he'd ever make.

As I rolled to my right onto my back to face him, I jostled my shoulder and saw stars from another sharp wave of pain shooting through my torso. It didn't stop me from firing and he hit the floor. I struggled to my feet and heard him moan. Towering over him I saw the tatts of Scarn space suits on his forearms. Then I was looking at a hole in his forehead and blood, bone, and brains on the floor through narrowed eyes.

A good part of the room was burning, and the fire was spreading to what wasn't. The searing heat, brilliant glow, and boiling smoke were making the place hell. It was time to get out.

I staggered out of the clubhouse, back into the refreshing night air. Feeling a bit light-headed and tired, I plopped down at a dumpster and sat with my back to it. A couple of coughs onto the back of my right hand spotted it and the .45 with blood. Shotgun pellets had nicked a lung.

The crackling and dancing flames of the fire were hypnotizing, and I realized I must have drifted off when voices nearby gave me a start. The crackling of the fire was still there, but it seemed more distant than before, and I couldn't see the flames although my eyes were open. I tried to lift the .45, but couldn't. It may as well have been a ton of bricks.

"I wonder if he did all this himself," a woman's voice said. She was very close.

"Don't know," a man answered. "However it got done, it's some mighty fine work. Mighty fine."

I recognized the man's voice. It was the sheriff. I felt the pistol being taken from my hand and pressure on my left shoulder, which didn't hurt at all.

"It looks bad," the woman said. "He's lost a lot of blood."

She sounded as if she was in a distant well, and the crackling of the fire seemed to be dying out.

The memory of the bikers, their clubhouse, and the gun battle intruded on what I then realized was a dream of my boyhood home in Kansas City, and my eyes fluttered open. I was in the bedroom of a house. Through a window I saw the sun bathing a green field, and thick bandages that could have been mistaken for a football shoulder pad covered my left shoulder.

"He's awake," a loud voice called out.

I glanced in the direction of the sound and saw someone walking away from the door. Within a minute the sheriff came in. He had a quizzical expression on his face, as if he didn't know what to make of me.

"How do you feel?" he asked.

"Fine, I guess." My voice sounded weak.

"Good. You're in my home. You're a tough old bird according to the doc and you'll make it."

"Thanks for taking me in."

"You got all but two of the bikers. Those two boys ran. You know, what you did was mighty idiotic."

I put the expression on my face that went with a shrug and did manage to shrug my right shoulder.

"It was mighty inspirational though," he added.

It was surprising, but I didn't feel inspired or even any of the satisfaction I'd expected beforehand. "I take no pleasure from it."

"That's good. It was necessary, but killing people, even Scarn flunkies, should never be easy or enjoyable. You should know you haven't been connected to any of it."

"How'd that happen?"

"In normal times you would have been. You used your friend's truck and your weapons. But the two remaining bikers ain't Mensa members. Hell, none of them were. I submitted a report dated a week ago about the truck being stolen and planted your weapons in the home of a man who'd just died. I doctored his death certificate to say he died of a gunshot wound. And we have it in the records that you were hurt in a tractor accident burying dead animals."

"Thanks, but why?"

A wistful look came over the sheriff's face. "You know, I dream of a day when the Scarn are beaten. My grandchildren or great grandchildren will make it happen. They'll learn about the Scarn and their technology and then kick the bastards back to wherever they come from."

He stopped and looked at me for several seconds, as if studying my face for indications of character.

"I'm setting up a resistance cell here," he continued, sounding as if it was an ordinary thing. "You have guts and scientific training. And you're a little crazy. You're just what we need. Do you want to join up?"

The sheriff watched my face while I thought for a short time. There wasn't any downside. "Hell, why not."

"Welcome to the resistance." He had a toothy grin on his face.

"What would have happened if I'd said no?"

"Two Scarn came the day after your raid to look at the clubhouse and meet the two surviving bikers. The Scarn didn't seem to care a bit about the dead. All they did was tell the two left to populate the gang again. I wonder if the Scarn figured all you'd done was get rid of a bunch of weak overseers for them. But if the Scarn think that way, they're wrong. You've given us a chance to get some of our people into the gang. It's a good start."

He'd ignored my question on what would have happened if I'd said no. I didn't press. I could guess the answer.

He left to let me get some rest. I was embarrassed that I'd so misjudged him the first time we met. He was no country bumpkin, no do-nothing hick. Later I wondered what it would be like being a resistance fighter.

The Medium and the Message

Aliens are
trying to communicate
they rearrange
magnetic letters
on the fridge

"Honey,
what does
'Lake u5 toy our lead'
mean?"

in desperation
playing a riff on
the old crop-circle technique
of their reckless youth

alas, defeated by a coarse medium
and running out of shrubs

Finally
Mind control!
one of the humans
has become their unwilling
servant
he will do anything they ask
anything in his power
to hasten their conquest
of the Earth!

"Darling,
don't throw food!
What's got into you?"

— David C. Kopaska-Merkel

Star Song of the Granger

Long have rows of intangible oars swam
Within the aether luminiferous
Through the bright constellation of the Ram
Buffeted by a cosmic wind furciferous

To me alone belongs a ten thousand year charge
To tame a planet yet uncharted and unknown
I will freely roam through the barren fields at large
To finish with a full and verdant garden sown

Singular and solitary: There will be none other than I through these
years
Hark! As the planet bare and cold comes to view, my ship descends and
my long tillage nears

Breaking the ground is my initial task
Preparing it for plants and things that creep
While beneath the blue-white sun's light I bask
Drinking of the warmth until it sinks deep

I am a thing immortal and undying
Fit for aeons tilling my plantation ecumenical
The years, they leave me without even a slight sighing
But the soft whining of my parts mechanical

To this wild planet I am an alien sight: A foreigner, a stranger
But it shall grow accustomed to my sight as the ceaseless and enduring
granger

A century passes in what seems a blink
But ten fly by to me even quicker
Finally, I now can joyfully think
That the fields have never grown thicker

It is a world in a state of transformation
And my efforts have left their mark indelible
Now before my sight there is confirmation
This job was not a dream, yet still incredible

Ten times more my work needs still be completed 'fore my agrarian
charge's end
No longer alone, for countless hands of new creatures now help to my
planet tend

I have reached the ten millennia mark
Species abundant with my care now thrive
Indeed the wastes have become as a park
The sterile land now brims with things alive

But where are the cosmic vessels of my masters?
I wait for them with hope, but see not their ships' bow
Do they wish to not come to see my green pastures?
I suppose I must simply return to the plow

I tell myself: It is silly to expect such a rigid punctuality
In truth, I need only sustain a few more years in all actuality

They never came, I have waited the years
And all the stars I watched have strangely died
This bizarre sight stirs the depths of my fears
But to my task I shall always abide

For what is a million years to one made such as I?
Or if even longer than that, still more the same?
Life is a treasure: I shall not allow it die
It does not matter at all that they never came

But ever I sing to the stars which remain: To Deneb, Vega, and Altair
If man yet swims through the depths of the void, I pray he find the
land I planted here

— James Frederick William Rowe

Dear Cthulhu

by
Patrick Thomas

Dear Cthulhu,

I have a problem. My big sister is obsessed with the eighties. I don't mean the decade. I mean, she's obsessed with men in their eighties.

A while back, she got in trouble with the law for selling pirate DVDs. I don't mean she pirated movies. She snuck up to our neighbor's window and filmed him dancing around naked with a parrot. Well, he wasn't exactly naked. He had a hat with a skull and crossbones, an eye patch and a hook. She made videos of him singing *It's a Pirate's Life for Me*, *Sixteen Men on a Dead Man's Chest* and, oddly enough, *All the Single Ladies*. I have to admit watching this man shiver his timbers was amusing, but I think she crossed the line by actually selling DVDs to people. The police agreed and got her under some Peeping Tom law. She got sentenced to five hundred hours of community service and started working in a nursing home near our house.

At first it seemed like a good thing. "Britney" had always been a bit of a self-centered twit. I can say that because I'm her sister and we have to share a room. She never really cared about anybody else but herself. Working in the nursing home seemed to change that. At first she was annoyed, but then she seemed to look forward to it. Britney said she was going to keep on volunteering even after she served her time. She even dumped her loser boyfriend which made Mom and Dad very happy. I mean, she was a senior and eighteen years old. It was about time she started shaping up.

Then one Saturday she came home, beaten and bruised. I wanted to take her to the hospital, but she refused. She didn't want Mom and Dad to know. I had to do her make up to hide a bruise on her face. She was hurting so bad, we stole one of Dad's Vicodin and gave it to her. While she was loopy from the drug, she told me what actually happened. Turns out for all the months she's been volunteering at the nursing home, she's actually been sleeping with the older men. Not just one or two, but every guy in the nursing home over the age of 80, including one in a

coma, although she swears for the time she was with him, he wasn't comatose.

The old geezers apparently really enjoy her company, so they've all kept their traps shut and don't seem to mind sharing her. She had a couple close calls, like with one guy who dislocated his total hip while they were getting busy. Another guy she thought died, but figures his pacemaker kicked in and brought him back.

What happened that Saturday was she was having her way with a guy who was 89 years old. She claims they were going at it hard—she says wrinkles turn her on. Ick. The thought of it makes me want to barf. They forgot to lock the room door and the guy's wife had come to visit. Apparently he liked his women younger as she was only 73. Upon finding Britney riding her hubby like a wrinkled manatee, she proceeded to beat the crap out of her with a cane. Sis says she barely made it out of there alive and with her clothes. The old woman almost caught her, but one of her other lovers stuck his walker out and tripped the old bitty.

Sis is worried that the old woman is gonna squeal on her. She's only got twenty-five more hours to serve out her sentence, but she's afraid to go back. She says she figures what she did is legal and okay because she's 18. I don't because I think it's disgusting.

She's begging me not to tell Mom. So far, I can't figure out a way to tell my mother that her daughter is dating a man old enough to be my Mom's grandfather. Or rather, a group of men who collectively are probably over a thousand.

Even worse, she asked one of the codgers to prom. She says he barely looks a day over seventy-five and he's willing to spring for a corsage, a limo, a bottle of Viagra and a case of condoms. I think it would be social suicide. I pointed out that everyone will talk about it in our town so much that she'll have trouble getting a job when she graduates. Or worse—she might kill one of them.

That didn't bother her too much. Sis told me that all the old guys said that they put her in their wills. She figured if they went, she'd get a big payout. I told her that was doubtful at best, unless she saw it in writing. I'm only sixteen, but even I know that a guy will tell you anything to get into your pants. I doubt that changes just because he gets elderly. In fact, since the old and wrinkly are less likely to get any, they'd make their lies even bigger.

Britney wants me to tell her what she should do and I just don't know. Do you think the old woman squealed on her? Should she go back and try to get those last few hours in anyway? Should I tell my parents? And how do I talk her out of taking a guy with more wrinkles than a Shar-Pei to one of the most important social events of her life?

—Little Sister of Grandpa Chaser in Roanoke

Dear Roanoke,

Your sister is correct when she says it is legal. If she was under 18, the old men in question could be charged with statutory rape. Even though she's in high school, she is considered a legal adult and can make her own decisions, no matter how poor or warped they might seem to others.

Cthulhu endorses your take on the male of your species. Men as a whole will lie to the female of the species for even an outside chance at procreation. Although it sounds like your sister is more of a sure thing.

A woman scorned is capable of almost anything. Your sister should probably contact someone she trusts at the nursing home to see if the wife reported her yet. If she has, finish her hours elsewhere as they will likely ban her. If they press the issue, she can claim sexual harassment and threaten to sue. She can tell the men to back up her story if they ever want to procreate with her again.

If the old woman hasn't reported it, your sister should offer to make her a deal—if the wife keeps her mouth shut, your sister will stay away from her husband and not press assault charges against her. Then she should quickly finish her remaining hours on her sentence, being careful to avoid her recreational procreation partners, especially those who already have mates.

Assuming the men were actually telling the truth about their wills, there is also a problem with being written into a will for sexual favors. The family or heirs can use that information to tie up the money in court for years, so it could be a very long time before she sees any pay out.

As for the prom, Cthulhu agrees it is likely a poor social choice to attend with somebody more than four times her age. Her peers will likely not understand and taunt her over it. In the age of social media, she can be assured that pictures and video of her and her aged paramour will be posted online. However, depending on how outrageous, disgusting or promiscuous her behavior at the prom or on the dance floor is, there is always the chance that it could go viral. You mention your sister getting a job after high school, but made no mention of trade school or college, so she is headed for a menial job. Such exposure on the Internet could lead her to a sort of notoriety which might be parlayed into her so-called fifteen minutes of fame. She might become a spokeswoman for erectile dysfunction products or get a chance at a reality show. There is likely some network willing to air a show that starts out with a teen dating thirty old men and ends with one of them getting to date or marry your sister. If she decides to try each of them out in the bedroom, they should have EMTs standing by. If someone is overwhelmed by her procreation skills, it could be ratings gold.

At the very least, she could set up a website or dating profile listing her preference for old men. She will likely have no shortage of suitors. Instead of assuming she will be put into their will, she could ask for gifts in advance. This way she handles her perversion and provides for herself at the same time.

Dear Cthulhu welcomes letters and questions at DearCthulhu@dearcthulhu.com. All letters become the property of *Dear Cthulhu* and may be used in future columns. *Dear Cthulhu* is a work of fiction and satire and is © and ™ Patrick Thomas. All rights reserved. Any one foolish enough to follow the advice does so at their own peril. For more *Dear Cthulhu* get the collections *Dear Cthulhu: Have A Dark Day, Dear Cthulhu: Good Advice For Bad People,* and *Cthulhu Knows Best* from Dark Quest Books. Learn more at www.dearcthulhu.com.

The Storm People

Story by C.J. Killmer
Illustration by Tom Kelly

The sinister rumble of distant thunder made my heart pummel my chest from the inside with an ever-increasing tempo, made my blood box my ears, made adrenalin shoot like cold, electric Freon through my veins. Storms always did that to me, ever since I was thirteen.

I took another sip of my beer, savoring the delicious bitterness of it, and held the 12-gauge in my arms like a newborn. I was sitting Indian-style in a corner on icy tiles, my back to the wall—literally and figuratively. Despite the air conditioner blasting and the ceiling fan whirring at high speed above me, my clothes were damp with sweat. I couldn't help jumping at each sound I heard. It took all of my self-control to refrain from shooting at each noise—I had almost fired off a few rounds of buckshot when the A/C compressor had kicked on a little while earlier—but I wanted to make absolutely sure of my targets before I use up my ammo. I knew they'd come for me, and I wanted to be ready for them.

My name is Ed Gaines. I'm originally from Coral Gables, a nice old neighborhood that's right next to the city of Miami. I'm thirty-nine years old as of a couple of weeks ago, and I had good reason to believe it would be my last night alive.

It all had to do with storms—storms and the things that came with them, that lived in them and rode in them.

My grandmother first told me about the Storm People when I was six. She said the Storm People were creatures that lived in hurricanes and other big storms. They had wings and flew as fast as lightning on the gales. According to her, they were mischievous—but not in the cutesy, folksy Irish leprechaun or Norwegian troll sort of way. More like low-ranking, adolescent demons.

When Grandma first told us this, my twin brother Dave and I did not know how to take it. We had both recently discovered that Santa Claus, the Tooth Fairy, and the Easter Bunny were all just Mom, and these Storm People sounded no less bogus to us. If anything, they sounded even more implausible.

But Grandma was deadly serious.

"I'm not making this up, boys," she said. "If I am, may God strike me dead and my soul never reach Him." This statement immediately caught our attention, as Grandma was very religious, not prone to saying such things lightly. She was also highly educated for a woman of her generation; despite her strong faith, she didn't believe in any old-fashioned superstitions, like a lot of our friends' grandparents

did. She seemed to be telling the truth—or, at least, she believed she was. Even though we were still young, Dave and I had a vague notion that some old people weren't completely in touch with reality. We shared a look and I could tell he was worrying, as I was, that perhaps Grandma was becoming one of those old people.

"I've seen them," she continued. "During big storms. Mostly hurricanes, but sometimes the rougher tropical storms, too. They don't come in every storm, though. Never could figure out why sometimes they're there and sometimes not—you know, if there is some sort of pattern."

She said that often the Storm People actually caused more damage than did the storm itself. When the Storm People didn't show up, people were often shocked by how little damage even a major storm could cause. If, on the other hand, they showed up in force, they could make even a category-one hurricane into a massively destructive event.

"What do they look like?" Dave asked. He didn't sound like he believed her.

The Storm People were very dark gray, she told us, almost black but not quite, which helped them to blend in with the clouds through which they flew. They had small horns like a mountain goat and big, bat-like wings. She said that their eyes glowed a bright yellow-green, and that was the best way to spot them when they were zipping around in the storm clouds.

"When was the last time you saw one?" Dave asked, still sounding skeptical.

Grandma leaned back in her easy chair. "Hmm … Let's see … Must've been just before you two were born. Your birthday is in July; must've been the hurricane in June of that year. I remember, because I remember your mother looking ready to burst with you two boys when the storm hit.

"Ever since I found out about them, I never could help myself when a storm comes—I *have* to look for the Storm People. It's a compulsion. But you have to make sure that if you're looking for them, they can't see *you*. You've got to do it from a safe place. I used to look out this tiny window at our old house—this was back when your grandpa was still alive, and we still lived in our big old place down in Homestead. There was a little window in the garage, maybe four or five inches square, and I used it to peek out for the Storm People during the hurricanes. Nice and secure way to do it—they weren't likely to spot me, and even if they did, they couldn't get through that little hole. I saw them. Don't know if they could see me. I don't think so. I saw them several more times after that, and all the times I made sure they couldn't reach me, and I tried to make sure they couldn't see me. But there's no way to know for sure if they can see you—unless you ask them, of course. And I wasn't about to do that." She laughed, nervously.

She said that she knew we didn't believe her, and that she had been like us when her father had told her, back when she was about our age. But, she said, once she'd seen them, she'd believed.

For about a year after Grandma had told us about them, Dave and I, despite our skepticism, scrutinized every storm that hit Miami for a glimpse of the Storm People. Grandma had put on a pretty convincing front. We never saw them, though, and before we turned ten we had for practical purposes forgotten all about the Storm People.

We rarely discussed them—or why Grandma had fed us such B.S. Neither of us—not even Dave, who was the biggest monster movie fan in the world—believed my grandmother's stories until we saw a Storm Person for ourselves.

This would have been when I was thirteen. One month after we both turned thirteen, the biggest of the many hurricanes I went through as a child hit south Florida. Grandma had been dead for two years by then. My Dad had been gone for as long as Dave and I could remember; he and Mom had divorced and he went, I always heard, out West to Idaho or Utah or someplace like that.

So it was just me, Dave, and Mom in the house. As the storm approached, the three of us did our best to board up the windows, but we didn't finish all of them in time. Two small ones on the east side of the house, by the bedroom that Dave and I shared, remained un-shuttered.

"We'll just have to leave it, boys," Mom said. "Move anything valuable out of your room, and we'll all sleep in the living room tonight."

We weren't about to argue. The hurricane was moving in quickly, and the sun was setting, too. Besides, the three of us sleeping on couches and sleeping bags in the middle of the house sounded fun to Dave and me—kind of like camping.

None of us were really scared of storms—at least not back then—so the first half of the night *was* fun. Dave, Mom, and I stayed up listening to the wind and lightning, and we played cards, listened to the radio, told ghost stories, and ate junk food. Mom had several glasses of wine. Sometime after midnight, Mom told

us to go to sleep. She said that when we woke up in the morning, the storm would definitely be gone and we could go outside to check out the damage. Within minutes, Mom was snoring.

We'd been asleep for a while, maybe a couple of hours, when a loud bang of something hitting the walls of the house woke up Dave and me. Mom was still sleeping, snoring loudly.

"Maybe it's the Storm People," Dave whispered to me. I couldn't see him in the darkness, but I could tell by his tone that he was smiling. I could see it in my mind—Dave had this distinct smile, almost like an Elvis Presley sneer, but much friendlier looking. And his eyes would always twinkle, an effect only enhanced by the fact that his eyes were different colors. One was hazel, the other ice-blue. I was always jealous. Both of my eyes were ho-hum brown.

It took me a few moments to remember what Storm People were. "Yeah, right," I finally said, with as much sarcasm as I could muster.

"I'm gonna go look out our window," Dave said.

"I don't think that's a good idea. What if a tree branch or something comes flying through while you're there? You could really get messed up."

"Oh, come on, what are the odds? I'll just go look for a minute, just in case there are Storm People, see if Grandma was really full of shit or not." His voice still had the smiling tone to it. "You gonna come?"

"No."

"Wuss," Dave said, and I could hear him get up and walk slowly through the middle of the house towards our room. All was quiet for a minute or two, and I lay there hoping Dave would come back soon, preferably without a flying stop sign impaling him.

Then it happened, fast—glass shattering, Dave screaming, and a chilling, inhuman chuckle. I popped up out of my sleeping bag, and I heard the sofa's springs shift as Mom snapped out of her sleep.

"Oh shit," she said.

"What was that?" I whispered to her.

"Probably something hit one of the two windows in the whole damn house that aren't shuttered."

"Dave's in there!"

"What?!" She clicked on the electric lantern. I could hear her voice instantly sober up.

"And something was—I don't know, it sounded sort of like laughing, but not human. Like an animal," I said.

"What the hell are you talking about?" She was already striding fast towards our room, lantern in front of her. I followed.

When we reached my bedroom door, Mom stopped so suddenly that I ran full-speed into her back, lost my balance, and fell hard on my butt on the tile floor. As I grunted from the fall, my mother screamed in a way I've never heard before or since, starting quietly and then rising in volume until it seemed loud enough to break glass.

After what seemed like a long time but was probably only a few seconds, her scream died off and she ran into the room, shouting "Drop him! Get away from him!"

I picked myself up and looked into the room in the uneven light of the lantern, which Mom had dropped on the floor.

A Storm Person was there, standing by the window, dripping wet. It looked just like Grandma had described: shaped vaguely like a human with a muscular build, but with dark gray skin; small horns above its eyes, the same color as its skin; and big eyes that glowed as if they were made of firefly butts. The thing had leathery-looking wings folded up behind its back. It was holding my brother around the neck with one huge fist, and it looked poised to leap back out the window.

The scene seemed to be in slow-motion as I watched my mother pick up our Louisville Slugger from where it leaned against the wall. She charged the Storm Person, screaming and swinging. But she just wasn't quick enough. Before she could cross the room, the Storm Person leapt out through the broken window, out into the hurricane. Mom followed it out, and I followed her. We both cut our arms pretty badly on the remaining bits of glass, though we didn't even notice this until later.

The instant I hit the grass outside, a huge bolt of lightning lit up the black sky enough to see the Storm Person. It was rapidly ascending in spirals, already at least fifty feet into the air, with Dave still dangling from one of its hands.

Mom fell to her knees, crying and screaming "No" over and over. I clung to her like I was a baby again, crying just as hard as her. We both knew there was nothing we could do. Dave was gone.

By morning, the storm had abated and my mom's terror and rage had already mutated into bitter grief. She sat me down to talk. Fallen trees had blocked off our street, so we couldn't go anywhere for the time being. The phones were out at the moment, too, so she wouldn't be able to call the authorities to report Dave missing until they were fixed.

"I know I've always stressed honesty with you

and Dave." Mentioning his name made her voice tremble noticeably. "But we can't tell the truth about this. You understand, Eddie?"

I nodded.

"People would think we were crazy, or that I killed Dave, or something like that," she continued. "Hell, *I* never believed Grandma's crazy stories until last night. We can never tell anyone the truth about this. Understand?"

Again, I nodded.

We sat around the house in silence, in a daze the rest of the day until the phones came back on in the late afternoon. My mother called the police to report Dave missing, making up some story about him sneaking out of the house during the storm.

Mom lived another seven years until a heart attack killed her while I was a sophomore at the University of Miami. But most of the Mom I knew—the happy, upbeat person—had died the night the Storm Person took Dave, and her last seven years were mired by depression and heavy drinking.

I saw a Storm Person again when I was twenty-six. At the time I was renting an apartment in Saint Augustine and living with a girl named Violet, a red-haired, green-eyed beauty. I always thought Violet was much too beautiful and intelligent for a guy like me—a guy who considers himself painfully average on a good day. Most guys like me have had, if they're lucky and halfway decent at bullshitting, at least one girlfriend that they've felt was a bit above them. It's a weird situation because, on the one hand, you feel like you've really pulled one off; on the other hand, there's always that anxiety gnawing on your subconscious that she'll realize she's way above you and could do *much* better, and that'll be it, you'll be back to mediocre girlfriends again.

Besides being gorgeous, Violet was a genuinely nice, sweet person. She didn't poke any fun at my phobia of storms, the way I ran for cover at the slightest whiff of a thunderstorm, and the way I anxiously watched the Doppler images on the Weather Channel every time a major storm came anywhere near Florida—which was frequently.

I had told her about Dave. Not everything, of course. If I had told her about the Storm People, she'd probably have thought I was crazy and would have dumped me. Hell, I'd have done the same, had the situation been reversed. The Storm People are one of those things that you can't ever really believe in till you've seen them with your own eyes—and when that happens, you or someone close to you will usually be taken.

So I'd just told Violet that my brother had died in a big storm when we were kids, and she didn't press me for details and she never said anything derogatory or demeaning about my fear—'astraphobia,' Violet had told me. She was working on an advanced degree in psychology at the University of North Florida at the time, so she knew the technical term for fear of storms. To her, my fear was no different than a fear of heights or elevators—nothing unusual.

One night, after we'd been living together for several months, a storm hit. It wasn't really that bad—nowhere near hurricane strength—but of course I couldn't sleep. We'd rented some movies to watch— Violet had insisted, and it was a good idea. It did take my mind a little off my phobia. Not completely—that would have been impossible—but a little.

But then, around three in the morning, the power went out. I've never hated an organization as intensely as I hated Florida Power & Light that night. My hatred only intensified as the minutes ticked by and the power failed to come back on.

Violet was a good girlfriend, though. After the power had been out for maybe twenty or thirty minutes, she took my mind off the weather and the darkness. She lit some candles and we made love. I have to say it was one of the best times ever with her, and she was by far the most attractive and the most skilled lover I've been with in my life. It really did blank out my mind, shutting it up, even halting my involuntary phobia symptoms.

As we lay on the bed panting in the afterglow, a light sheen of sweat on both of us and a real smile on my face for the first time since I'd heard on the news that a big storm was headed our way, I heard a noise outside. The storm was loud, but still, it sounded like that same chuckle that had been burned into my memory from the night Dave was taken.

"Did you hear that?" I said.

"Hear what?"

"That laughing sound?"

"No," Violet said. "I can't hear anything but rain and wind and thunder. I don't know how you could hear anything over all that."

For a while I didn't hear anything else, and I started to relax a little, thinking it was just my imagination. In fact, I relaxed so much that I fell asleep, just blacked out into the beautiful smells and feels of Violet as she cuddled up against me.

How long I slept, I don't know. It might have been ten minutes, or it might have a couple of hours.

I'm not sure what actually woke me up—it might have been the sound of breaking glass, or maybe Violet had made a noise. All I know for sure is that I was jolted out of very deep sleep and immediately became aware of two things. The first was that Violet's body was no longer up against mine. The second was that the bedroom window nearest the bed was broken. Noise and water poured into the apartment.

I knew beyond any doubt that a Storm Person had snatched Violet away from me, out of my arms and into the storm. I started crying right away as I stood before the broken window, my tears blending seamlessly with the rain that lashed in at me. And I could've sworn that I heard Violet's screams—faintly, to be sure, and mostly drowned out by the storm— mixed with the laughter of Storm People; it sounded like there were several, somewhere up there in the dark clouds. Fear kept me from going outside to see if I could rescue her. Instead, like a coward, I huddled and wept underneath a blanket until the storm receded and dawn arrived.

I had the window fixed, and a few days later filed a missing persons report on Violet. I made up a story about her running an errand before the storm and never coming back. Not surprisingly, the police's investigation failed to yield any information on Violet's whereabouts—only the Storm People would know about that. I think they suspected me for a little while, but after a while they decided there wasn't any evidence to support that theory.

A few years later, I moved to Jacksonville, and had lived there ever since. For some reason, I couldn't leave Florida. I felt like if I did, the Storm People would have won some sort of victory. Besides, I was pretty sure they'd find me wherever I went.

After Violet was taken, I lived as a virtual hermit. I bought a little house on an acre of land in a rural part of neighboring Clay County. I didn't date, and got a night security job at the port where I would be unlikely to make any friends. I didn't want anyone close to me, because it seemed the Storm People were stalking them for some reason known only to them. I decided that if Storm People were going to come for anybody, it would be just me. Only this time, unlike the other times, I'd be ready.

I realized that the Storm People seemed to come in thirteen year intervals, and it just so happened that Dave and I were born on a year that they came, which was when Grandma had seen them. That was why we saw them for the first time when we were thirteen, and then I saw them again thirteen years later.

After I turned thirty-nine, I watched the weather report with even more than the usual apprehension. I always made sure that I had a firearm nearby any time a storm threatened. When the news began warning of an approaching tropical storm, I knew the time had come.

I put up my steel hurricane shutters and triple-locked my steel-reinforced front and back doors. As the dark clouds closed in, I barricaded myself in my bedroom along with a flashlight, some beef jerky, a cooler full of waters and beers, plus a Remington 870 riot shotgun with an attached flashlight and lots of spare shells. I loaded the shotgun's extended magazine tube with its full complement of nine rounds, alternating buckshot and rifled slugs. I had no idea if the gun would be enough when the Storm People came for me, but I was determined to kill as many of them as I could before they got me.

The waiting was absolute horror. I don't think I would have sweated as much if I had run a marathon in Miami in August. My nervous system was keyed up to its ultimate limits. I had never tried cocaine, but I imagined that if one took a massive, pure dose of it, the effects would be similar, only without the gut-pummeling terror.

As the storm moved in, and I heard the rain on the roof, and the wind rattling the shutters, and the thunder got louder and more frequent, my hands started to shake and I felt almost as if I were having a seizure. The terror was so intense I actually began wishing that the Storm People would show up, just so that the anticipation would be finished. I even began to contemplate turning the shotgun on myself.

But before I could make a decision on that possibility, something thudded into the rear of the house hard enough to shake the whole building. I had no doubt what it was.

Then it started bang on the walls, over and over. It was ten times louder than the thunder. I wanted to scream, I wanted to hide, I wanted to shut my eyes and make it go away. Instead, I picked up the shotgun, stuffed my pockets full of extra shells, and headed to the back door.

I unlocked all three of the locks and shoved the door open. Just as I stepped outside a flash of lightning illuminated the backyard, and I could see in detail what waited for me—a Storm Person. I felt the usual fear and revulsion, and stood frozen in front of the doorway, the shotgun's muzzle hanging down towards the ground, useless and forgotten. The Storm Person took a step towards me. It looked like it was relishing the moment.

I might have stood there, a fossil of fear, until it took me, but something snapped me out of the daze. In another flash of lightning, I got a clear look at the Storm Person's facial features—it was smiling a distinctive, sneering smile. It reminded me of Dave. I raised the shotgun and clicked on the attached flashlight, shining it in the Storm Person's face. In the split second before its hands came up to fend off the blinding LED light, I got a good look at its eyes—one hazel, one ice-blue. Somehow, they had turned Dave into one of them.

Then another Storm Person landed behind the first. This one looked female. Its body, though angular with muscle like all of them, still retained some curves around the hips and breasts. As it got closer, I could see a few strands of red hair fluttering between its stubby horns. And it had green eyes. Violet.

"Dave! Violet!" I shouted. "What happened? They turned you into *them*?"

Neither said a word. They just stared at me.

"It's me, Ed," I said. "Don't you recognize me?"

Still they stared. I saw not the slightest glimmer of recognition. Then the Storm-Person-who-had-been-Dave charged me. Instinctively I pointed and fired the shotgun, giving him a faceful of buckshot. He staggered, taken aback, but didn't fall. Inky black blood spurted from his wounds, glossy in the LED beam.

I pumped. The empty shell flew out and pinged off the wall. I pulled the trigger again. The slug impacted his chest and knocked him down in a puddle of black-oil blood. His legs twitched once, twice, then lay still.

I worked the action again. The Violet-creature was circling to the left, looking for an opening to pounce. I wasn't about to give her the opportunity. I gave her two in the chest and she went down, twitched, then stopped just as the Dave-creature had, a pool of black growing around her body.

I collapsed down onto the lawn hard as the rain continued to soak me. I thought I was going to faint, or maybe puke, but I didn't do either. Instead I looked up, into the storm. Rainwater poured into my eyes, but I didn't mind. Lightning flashed, and in its instantaneous illumination I saw black, winged figures swarming in the sky. I reloaded my shotgun with fumbling fingers and waited for them, resigned to die in a last stand. I felt like dying, since I had just killed what was left of two people I had loved.

But they never swooped down for me. Perhaps

they were scared to suffer the fate of their dead comrades. I took some small comfort in that.

How long I sat there outside in the storm, I'm not exactly sure. It must have been a while, because by the time I finally stood up, the storm was mostly gone and it was getting light.

When I did get up, I looked at the bodies of the Storm People. Only they weren't Storm People any more – there was my brother Dave, still thirteen years old. And there was Violet, still in her early twenties. They looked just as they had when they'd been taken. Both were naked, both were dead, and both were smiling. They had a look of peaceful rest that convinced me I had freed them by killing them. Somewhere deep inside those two Storm People there had still been some remnant of the people I had loved, and I had liberated them.

For the first time since my last night with Violet, I smiled.

I knew the authorities would never understand any of it, that they would just see me as some nut who'd murdered two naked people in my backyard. So I hid the bodies and left Florida for good. I ended up in Nevada. I took on a new name and started a new life. And on the rare occasions when storms come to my corner of the desert, I'm not scared anymore.

The Dream Eater

For some silver
He will eat
Your dreams.
A soft kiss
On the forehead,
Then a tremendous
Suck, it will
Leave a mark.
He prefers
Nightmares,
Says they have
A spicy taste,
But you must
Find him quickly,
He wants them
Fresh when they
Still have bite.

— K.S. Hardy

Upon Encountering Your Ghost

I,
  entering the dead-still
  but never calm
  or calming
  dream-pit of the night,
Walk empty,
  trash-strewn avenues
  and hunger for a glimpse
  of the eternal contradiction
  that you represent.

Yes I,
  who sought perfection,
  found it nowhere.

Least of all
  in the battered
  and decaying landscape
  of your soul.

And I ran,
  in abject terror,
  telling myself
  it was from
  the alcohol and the drugs
  that were already
  killing you.

It was all a lie,
  of course.

And you,
  tangled brown hair flying
  in a breeze I cannot
  bear to feel,
  now fix me
  with unblinking eyes.

The cobalt-blue darts
  of your fingernails
  plunge through
  my unresisting skin
  to shrivel
  what remains
  of my inner organs
  with the permafrost
  of abandonment and shame.

— Jim Lee

First published in *The Tome*, volume 2, issue #5, 1990.

Hair Raiser

Story by Ken Goldman
Illustration by Paul Niemiec

"What He hath scanted men in hair,
He hath given them in wit."
— William Shakespeare

Harry Gardner waited ten minutes into his act before breaking out the bad-ass material. He knew that when the hot stage lights shone off the beads of sweat on the top of his head, somehow the baldy jokes seemed funnier. Besides, the yuppie crowd expected the off-color chrome-dome routines that had become his trademark. Scanning the front tables of the Funny Bone Cabaret, Harry focused on the buxom blonde sipping wine and wearing a red dress with a neckline that plunged as far South as was legal.

"Hey! I caught you staring at my head! Tell me, honey, when you see all this bare skin in one place and then look down, do you get any sense of deja vu?" Although those who sat close to the stage knew they were open targets for the stand-ups, the woman's face flushed with embarrassment and her date suddenly took a keen interest in his cocktail napkin. Harry beaded in on the blonde. "So what's your name, honey? Raquel? Marilyn? Brunhilda?"

"Dolly," the blonde volunteered with a breathy shyness, and Harry could not have asked for a better response than if he had planted the woman there himself. The crowd went wild.

"Let me ask you something, *Dol*-ly ," he said stepping toward her, pointing to a set of pipes that practically spilled over the small table. "Don't you need a special zip code for those things?" He waited for the laughs to die down, then whispered into his mike as if sharing a secret with the howling audience, "I gotta check out this mama's bazooms for myself!" Several guys seated in the corner of the club hooted as the comic jumped from the stage while singing something about being "too sexy for my hair."

Harry headed for the couple's table and lowered his face to the young woman's cleavage, turning for a moment toward her date. "You don't mind my doing a little experiment with *Dol*-ly, do you … what'd you say your name was?" he asked the guy as he pressed his cheek against the soft flesh of the blonde's breasts.

"Bob," the guy said, clearly at a disadvantage.

"Bob! That's just what I intend to do, pal!" Harry said, and this line brought the house down. The woman's date sat mute and flustered, attempting a dopey grin while the comic maneuvered his bald head along the blonde's chest. Resting it beside her left breast, he looked up and offered her a toothy smile. "Honey,

you got hooters that match my hat size! I'll bet if I left my head here, in the dark old Bob would never know you didn't have three of them. Except, of course, 'till he discovered one of them bazongas could talk!"

The room exploded. Even the blushing woman's date grinned widely.

"No wedding bands?" he asked the guy, setting up the poor slob for the kill. "Then you'll enjoy this next part!" The comic pulled off his tie and blindfolded the young woman's date, who had suddenly taken on the look of an animal caught in the headlights of an oncoming truck. "Now, Bob, what I want you to do *first* is to rub the top of my head. And *then* what I want you to rub is—"

The room thundered with pee-in-your-pants laughter. This bit never failed to fracture the crowd. Four hundred people roared at the comic's shining bald head and the humiliation of the hapless schmuck named Bob he had forced to rub it.

The blonde did not miss a beat. At the height of the laughter she shoved a small sealed envelope into Harry's palm, and the twinkle in her eye said it all. She had timed the move so perfectly the crowd roared even louder. Pretty shrewd on her part, the comic thought. Get the attention off the poor schmuck's dilemma while he's blindfolded, and at the same time slip the headliner her phone number. He had underestimated this one. He smiled back at her, winked at the crowd, and slipped the envelope into his pocket.

Harry savored the moment. Once they turned off the stage lights there were not a whole lot of them worth savoring.

* * *

Offstage Harry was just another paunchy guy with enough hairs on the top of his head to tote on his fingers. He had always considered his baldness an omen, because whatever had been meaningful in his life had departed with his hair before he turned thirty. That included his marriage and most of his worldly possessions. But his shiny scalp was good for a few laughs on the comedy circuit, and in time the comic developed a stoic attitude about having a head that looked like a penis that had been kept in cold storage. Laughter was the best laxative, he told himself, and if life had tossed him a lemon he would make lemonade. Then he would piss in it.

"*Hey, last week I went to a rabbi and the man tried to circumcise my head!*" Drummer, a rim shot, please. Ba-ba-boom!

"*Hey, don't call me bald. I'm follicly impaired!*" and

segue into the tit jokes.

"Lady, are those your tits or did you sneak two short bald-headed men into my show?" Shoot down a bimbo or two, applause and exit.

The three comedians appearing at The Funny Bone each shared the same small dressing room, but no stand-ups who played The Bone ever expected it to be Vegas. The other two who had gone on before Harry were new kids with starry-eyed girlfriends wetting their panties from the comped seats. The freshman class of jokesters was so green that for their one shot onstage Tony Morelli, who managed the place, usually made them grab brooms after the show. Many asses got kissed in this business, but Harry had passed his pucker-up phase years ago. He told Morelli that any ass he kissed would have to come fully assembled with tits like melons, a beaver pit that tasted like strawberry ice cream, and a mouth that could suck the chrome off a Buick.

Harry sat alone in the dressing room thinking about the blonde, and searched his shirt pocket for the envelope she had shoved into his hand during his show. "Well, Hello Dolly!" he sang, and tore the envelope open. He read it and the smile melted from his face.

"Fuck!" he muttered to himself.

The woman had slipped him a business card that read **BALD MEN! HAVE HAIR NOW! Not a wig! Not a transplant! Call HAIR TODAY at 476-2000 for appointment!** This time the joke was on him. The blonde had gotten the last laugh with her own baldy joke, and this punch line was a corker. Crumpling the card in his fist Harry noticed the small print in the corner and unraveled it in his palm. **This procedure is absolutely free!**

"Yeah, right!" he growled under his breath, then stopped himself just before he tossed the card into the ash tray. The thought hit him like a cold slap. Suppose she had given him the number where she worked? Suppose ol' Dollytits had been on the level? Hell, even if she were just playing a fast set of mind-fuck with him, he knew how to rush the blonde's net. He did it for a living.

Harry made the call to Hair Today the next morning. An answering tape with a breathy woman's voice responded by asking him to leave his name and to select any Wednesday morning for an appointment during working hours. He wondered if the voice belonged to the blonde. She had said only a few words during his act, and if she were like most women she had probably been too flustered to speak in her

most natural voice with a spotlight shining down her cleavage. There was no way to know if she were the same woman.

But just in case the voice on the tape belonged to the blonde, Harry intended to play this game to win. He waited for the beep, then made the appointment for Wednesday without even going for a punch line. He was smiling when he hung up.

Somewhere in a dark corner of his brain he heard a drummer doing a rim shot.

* * *

No address had appeared on the crumpled card. The next morning there came a short return call of confirmation in the same recorded voice spoken by the same breathy woman. The recording confirmed the time of the appointment, gave the address and office number with no attempt at directions, and within fifteen seconds after Harry had picked up the receiver, the message cut off. Hair Today clearly did not give a rat's turd for formalities.

When Harry's cab arrived at The Harbor Towers Medical Building off Pratt Street, Hair Today regained some credibility, even if its location was not in the most fashionable section of the Inner Harbor district. He had half expected the driver to drop him at a massage parlor near the Baltimore bus terminal, and had that occurred the busty blonde could have claimed game, set, and match. But that had not happened, and as Detective Holmes might say, the game was still afoot.

This game was a head game, and in more ways than one. Before anyone began planting hairs into Harry's head he intended to get a proper introduction to the slippery blonde. He had come this far, and if that cock teaser were anywhere inside the Harbor Towers, by nightfall her titties were going to come out and say howdy. He took the elevator to the sixteenth floor expecting a sign on the door to indicate Hair Today's office, but the door contained only the name of Dr. D. Manning, Dermatologist.

The real surprise waited behind the door.

"Hello, Mr. Gardner," the woman seated at the computer terminal said. "We've already met. I'm Dr. Manning. Darlene Manning. My friends call me Dolly." The blonde woman stood and offered her hand, and Harry seemed unsure about what to do with it before he shook it. "Heard any good tit jokes lately?" she asked.

Harry's tongue felt nailed to his jaw. "Listen, I didn't mean—"

"—It's okay, really," she continued, removing her

glasses. "This isn't The Funny Bone and you don't have to make me laugh. Let's not kid each other, Mr. Gardner. I know why you came and what you really want. But you have something that I want too, and maybe we can help each other. You see, I really am a dermatologist, licensed and everything," she explained as she pointed to the diploma on the wall from the University of Maryland Medical College. "And you might say I selected you before you selected me. That's why I slipped you the note."

"Call me Harry," he said as he followed her into the inner office. The woman was one of those night creatures who by daylight metamorphosed into a proper businesswoman, but even her white lab coat could not hide those speed bumps. She went to a small freezer, pulled out a tray, and placed it on the lab table. Four styrofoam head shells were inside the tray, and on each head rested what appeared to be four wigs of varying color and in bad need of combing.

"Select one," she said.

"Look, Doctor … Darlene. I'm not really the wig type," Harry answered, aware of his sudden embarrassment. "I wore a rug once, and it looked like road kill that had climbed on my head and died there."

"These aren't wigs, Harry. I'm a dermatologist, not a beautician. And generally you don't keep wigs in the freezer. You see, this is living, growing hair."

Harry knew when someone yanked his chain, and this bitch-kittie was trying to pull it from the socket. "Yeah, I hear styrofoam is real good at stimulating those follicles. Okay, you had your laugh, Doctor. I'm sorry about the tit jokes the other night, but it's my job, you know? And—"

"—Harry, this is no joke," she interrupted. The woman picked up a styrofoam head. "I'll give you the layman's explanation, and if you still want to walk, I'll open the door for you. Look closely at the styrofoam, Harry, where the hair is attached. That's a thin epidermal layer of skin taken from the scalp of a cadaver. When I inserted these hair follicles two weeks ago, they were no longer than maybe a quarter of an inch."

Harry looked at the hair that spilled over the styrofoam head. It looked like it could have been shorn off the head of a heavy metal rock star. He examined the hair closely, ran his fingers through it. It felt as if the roots had embedded themselves right into the styrofoam.

"You see, Harry, hair still grows after one dies, maybe for several days. These hair samples were taken from morgue specimens while it was still growing. I treated the follicles and inserted them into a thin layer of skin taken from the scalp of the same cadaver."

"Treated the follicles?" Harry asked. "Doctor, you're beginning to sound like the demon child of Victor Frankenstein and Sy Sperling."

The joke went unacknowledged. "With a conventional hair transplant, the donor hair is taken from your remaining hair, then plugged back into your head in the area where it's needed. But the result is often disappointing, because the donor area itself is sparse, the hair thin, and plugs don't always take. Often a patient's head winds up looking like a dart board."

Harry smiled. "The lady made a joke!" he said, but the woman did not return his smile.

"This procedure requires no donor area taken from the patient's head. As much hair as needed can be added and it will grow because of the treatment given it. You see, Harry, Hair Today has discovered a way to regrow living hair, hair that is not taken from the same bald donor. Did you know, minoxidil was originally intended as a treatment for hypertension? It was only by accident that dermatologists discovered it could also regrow hair. The formula, polydermal retin-9, was meant to restore healthy skin where skin had been damaged, as with burn victims. Instead we discovered PDR-9 could restore hair! Look at the third shell in this tray, Harry."

She picked up the styrofoam head that was covered in thick black hair.

"Elvis, right?" said Harry.

The woman again disregarded the joke. "This hair was grey, almost white. After the treatment it turned jet-black, its original color, and regained its thickness. Harry, this hair did not merely go through a color change. It *regenerated* ! And it did so while growing on a dead man's scalp attached to styrofoam! After treatment, the follicles simply took root and grew. Just attached themselves to that scalp like they were on a feeding frenzy. That hair grew almost a quarter of an inch a day in normal temperatures; grew so fast it became unruly. That's why these specimens are kept in the freezer. And hair placed on a bald scalp treated with PDR-9 can just as easily grow on a man's head. Or on *your* head!"

"Let me guess," Harry interrupted. "You're not only the president, you're also a client?"

The woman blushed, and ran her fingers through her hair. "No, this is my hair. That man you saw me with at the comedy club, Bob, helped provide the funding through the Maryland Research Foundation. But I *am* the 'president', so to speak. In fact, I'm Hair Today, period. Chairman of the board, Chief

Researcher, office manager, and coffee maker. This is going to be very big, Harry, and that's why I've been offering the process at no cost to bald men who are, in some way, in the public eye. I've targeted my control group as males whose words carry some weight, Harry, and you fit that profile."

"And what profile is that, Doctor? Hairless or dickless? Look, if you really want a shot at my gonads there are easier ways of getting to them. I'm just a guy trying to earn a few—"

"—Harry," she interrupted. "I admit I never saw much funny about misogynists with good punch lines, but in this case I'm a doctor, not a woman. We're talking about a scientific breakthrough, nothing else. Just see this in practical terms, Harry. No woman alive is unaware of that all-powerful male ego, yet all women are drawn to powerful men. Ever since Sampson a man's power has been directly tied to his hair. Hair is power, Harry, don't you see? It's like the male peacock's plumage, a law of nature. The lady peahen is a sucker for the cock's feathers."

"So we're talking about cock sucking?"

"*Power*, Harry, that's what we're talking here," she emphasized, and made a fist. She seemed to catch herself, and her voice softened. "Look, there's no hard-sell here. If the procedure doesn't work, if the hair doesn't implant itself, you've lost nothing. But if it *does* work on you and other men like you…"

"How many other 'public figures' have agreed to this procedure?" Harry asked.

"Counting you?" she asked, and smiled unconvincingly. "…One."

"Sorry, Doctor," Harry said. "Elvis has left the building. You might want to consider returning his hair."

He headed toward the door, but she called his name and something in that breathy voice stopped him cold. He turned to her and noticed she had removed her lab coat. "Harry, why don't we discuss this just a little longer?"

She smiled at him as she began to unbutton her blouse.

* * *

Harry Gardner was not a religious man, and the only times he had ever willingly set foot inside a church had been his wedding day and the afternoon of his mother's funeral. But on the floor of Dr. Darlene Manning's office, with the hard-bodied dermatologist squirming under him, Harry Gardner spoke to God. He signed the papers for the PDR-9 procedure before he had his pants back on. He would have jumped into a tub filled with the stuff for another go-round with that woman.

Sliding back into her lab coat the blonde doctor again became all business. She explained that 'treated' hair was somewhat different from normal hair. At room temperature PDR-9 made hair grow faster, and unless Harry planned to visit the barber once a week he would have to sleep with a specially made cap that produced cold temperatures and kept the hair growth in check during the night. Harry told her he could live with that.

The doctor wasted no time. The following morning she smeared Harry's head with the muddy liquid as if she were basting a Christmas turkey. The gunk felt warm and sticky, and the woman worked without saying a word. The process involved no elaborate transplant procedures, no needles because the hair follicles had been treated with the same formula that she had smeared on his scalp. She placed several small square-inch patches of thick black hair upon the areas she had smeared, working slowly so each hair would take root at the proper angle to assure that all-important natural hairline. From start to finish, the entire procedure took less than three hours.

Together they waited for the follicles to embed themselves into Harry's scalp. The woman stood over him observing the top of his head with a small pocket flashlight, tamping out the thin trickles of blood resulting from the follicles entering the scalp, and occasionally jotting down notes.

After another hour she asked, "Ready to look?" and Harry simply nodded back. He was tired of sitting while unable to scratch his itching scalp, and could think of no punch line appropriate for the moment.

But when she held the mirror to his face, Harry's words caught in his throat. An image of his high school yearbook picture flashed through his mind, back when he used to wear his hair in a razor sharp crew cut to stand out from the freaks who buried their heads under self-righteous moss-like manes. The woman had given him back ten years of his life. Funny how she had told him about hair and ego, hair and power, because he had not come this close to humility in a long time.

"Doctor," he finally said, "I think I want to have your baby."

For the first time she returned his smile. "Thank you, Harry. But from where I'm standing it looks like you've just done that."

Harry canceled his bookings for three weeks. Dr. Darlene/Dolly Manning had suggested he consider deep-sixing the 'tit bits' that had been in his act because the old 'head-of-skin-like-your-boobs' routines were never very funny to most intelligent women anyway, and they weren't likely to get laughs when delivered by a stand-up who now had hair like Axl Rose. The doctor had a point. On his third visit to her office he promised if she came to the Laff House in Washington to watch the debut of his new act, he would lay off the tit jokes.

Although his new hair had grown like a weed, Harry had no desire to cut it. By show-time at the Laff House the thick black hair had already spilled over his ears and covered the nape of his neck. Harry knew the look was more '60's than New Millennium, but no one would ever tell him again that his neck looked like it had been getting a hard-on.

He stepped up to the mike onstage wearing a Baltimore Orioles cap and delivered a few standard one-liners to ready the crowd for his moment of truth. It was a good crowd, and they laughed in all the right spots. Any stand-up worth pocket change had to play an audience the way a concertmaster played a violin, and tonight Harry was a virtuoso.

During his opening bits he surveyed the tables inside the darkened room. There was a full house, maybe over five hundred out there, but Harry could not spot the beautiful blonde doctor. He had told the pimply kid out front to comp Dr. Darlene Manning and whomever came in with her. But it was a Saturday night, and Phil Goldfine, the little putz who ran the place, probably had sat them in the back. No matter, Harry thought. Feeling this good, he knew he could make the lady cream her pantyhose from two hundred feet.

"Well, I guess I can't hide my secret from you people any longer. See, I used to be really self-conscious about being bald, so I did something about it," he began. He removed the baseball cap and mounds of dark hair spilled out from under it. "My head has finally reached puberty!" he shouted. The crowd offered him polite laughter, but this joke was meant only as a set-up for the next few. "My friends tell me my transplant looks pretty good. The only trouble is, I can't find the hair around my balls!" This line scored a direct hit, and another crowd was in his pocket.

The stage lights baked his scalp, and Harry felt an uncomfortable tingling. But he always worked up a sweat onstage and had learned to roll with it.

"It's kind of weird," he continued, "but ever since I got these hair plugs my cat keeps shitting on my head." Two for two, and again thunderous laughter

followed. This crowd was the kind any comic would take home and sleep with.

(*…but damn those lights were hot!*)

The tingling sensation suddenly felt like a dozen bee stings, even worse than the first time the bodacious Dr. Manning had stood over him watching the hair follicles embed themselves in his scalp. But there was a show to do and jokes to tell, and timing was everything. Harry hoped the pain did not show on his face.

"Of course … It doesn't work when I ask my dates if they'd like to run their fingers through my hair anymore…"

(*Those lights are so fucking HOT!*)

"…because my toupee is … I mean, because I used to keep my hair in a box … near my bed … in case they wanted to do that."

His timing was off and the audience answered with silence, the nightmare of every stand-up comic who ever lived. The room suddenly seemed to tip to one side, then to another. The stage lights felt like they were burning a hole directly into his skull. The heat made Harry forget the next joke and the floor seemed to buckle under him. He had been thrown off, and he struggled to recover.

"Hey, lady!" he shouted to the skinny red head seated directly below the stage. "Add my head to your tits, and you're still short one tit!"

Damn! That was a baldy joke. Who's going to laugh at—?

Silence again, the kind that followed only funeral services and shitty jokes. The carrot-top bitch was not even smiling, and her mouth opened wide as if she were about to scream.

A thick black curtain suddenly blocked Harry's vision. For a moment he thought someone had finally turned off those damned stage lights. But the heat still blistered his scalp, and he realized that his hair had fallen into his eyes. He ran his fingers through it to push it back, and suddenly his mouth went dry and he found it hard to breathe

His hair had spilled over his entire face. It had grown several inches in the few minutes since he had stepped onstage. He turned his back on the crowd and tore through it with all ten fingers, stuffing it under his shirt collar. When he faced the audience again a woman seated near the stage screamed. Harry looked at his hands.

His fingers were drenched in blood. His face was streaked with thin rivulets of it dripping from his scalp. A guy in the back laughed, probably thinking this was part of some grotesque comedy bit, but already people in the front were leaving their seats and backing away from the stage.

"Jesus!" Harry screamed. "What the fuck is hap—?" A lightning bolt of pain stabbed at his brain and a thick gout of blood rolled into his eye.

The heat from the stage lights was making his hair grow!

Sharp pains jolted his head like electric currents, and Harry suddenly realized what was happening. The hair was not only growing *out* of his head. He could feel the hair growing *into* his head, the follicles boring their way through his skull as if…

…as if they were on a feeding frenzy!

"Turn off the goddamned lights!" he screamed while his knees struck the floorboards. The stage suddenly snapped into darkness. Harry felt his brain being chewed, and hot blood trickled from each ear while his head pulsed as if pricked from the inside by needles. He slid to the floor still holding the hand mike, gurgling blood into it as a thousand hair follicles planted themselves into his brain.

The lights in the club came on and the entire audience was on its feet, those in the rear pushing toward the stage to get a better look, those in front backing away. The club's bartender climbed onstage in time to see a dense clump of hair that had already gnawed its way through Harry's frontal lobe. It protruded in thick tufts from one of his eye sockets.

"Mr. Gardner, just lie still. We'll find a doctor," the guy said, trying hard not to gag at the bleeding pulp that remained of the comic's face.

Harry heard only one word. *Doctor.*

"I'm a doctor," said the buxom blonde in the red dress who knelt beside the twitching body on the floor that lay covered in mats of blood-soaked hair. The woman looked up at the small circle of wide-eyed onlookers that had come onstage. "Back off! This man needs air!" she shouted, then leaned forward as if to administer CPR to the comic gasping for breath and choking on mouthfuls of blood. Instead she moved her lips close to the comic's ear and whispered words meant only for him, the last words Harry Gardner would ever hear before his brain filled to bursting with thick heaps of jet-black hair.

"Hello, Harry," the woman whispered with her soft, breathy voice. "Heard any good tit jokes lately?"

First published in *Black Moon* #95, April 1996.

Illustration by Jag Lall

Praying You Won't Bite My Head Off

Always in that dream,
the mantis grinned at me,
having mated
and eaten her mate —

same way you grinned at me
when I said, "I do."
Grinning when I couldn't sleep;
grinning when they took me away.

Even now, guiltless
or devious,
you come to visit
grinning still.

And they wonder
why I am screaming.

— Lauren McBride

Gimme Shelter

Story by Douglas Empringham
Illustration by Laura Givens

Colby, near the end of his diurnal seclusion, tuned in a few sounds outside. From one direction came the freeway's hum of tires and blare of horns. Another compass point sent erratic tapping, as if someone was driving tent pegs. Attending this sound was the panicky squeals of rats scattering in disorder.

With a mild effort the vampire listened to their chittering. An enemy was in the junkyard. The taps were gunshots. But as bullets were no threat to him, he was indifferent to the rats' fate—though they were useful minions on occasion.

Colby stretched. His current lair was a van with a black denim and leather interior. Its final ride had ended when it rammed an unmovable concrete abutment doing 90-plus mph. An encounter that collapsed the front end as if an accordion. "Squashed 'em like bugs," the old junkyard owner had told him. The sweet odor of blood was part of the ambience.

Presently the shooter stopped and the resident guard dogs growled. But were given no command, though someone on the freeway border was climbing the sagging rusty link fence. Colby next heard running, one foot shoeless. A sound that entered the aisle outside his lair. Run, stop, run, stop. Then the runner clambered up a stack of auto bodies across from the van.

Colby fetched the smoky glass he'd salvaged from a welding mask and went to the nearer port. Two more runners became audible, the first in sneakers and the other in boots. As they approached he lifted a corner of the black curtain and peered through the dark glass.

The *hare* was now perched atop a teetering and shifting pile of vehicle shells. A squat, ruddy, red-haired young man unknown to Colby. His desperate run had left him with a torn windbreaker, stained jeans and only one cross-trainer.

"Keep running, Mark," the hare called down, "or you'll give me away."

Colby knew the first *hound*. Thin, androgynous, olive complexion, and in his late teens. That day he was tricked out in a thrift shop ensemble of orange sateen shorts, chartreuse basketball jersey, no sox and pink Keds. The uniform lacked either a player or a school name, and the number double zero had been added with mismatched characters.

Mark did not look up but he also did not keep running. Then Colby heard him whisper, "I don't owe you nothin', Sam."

The second hound arrived too winded to speak. Colby knew Reech. The dealer and pimp had offered him a joint and a place to crash. He was in his signature black boots, jeans, Henley shirt and leather biker vest. He was perhaps thirty and had heavy brows and a hooked nose. If you gazed into his eyes long enough, you saw the predator lurking within. When he could speak, he told the hare, "You're weak, Sam! A *loser!* Y're comin' on like y're some kinna superhero, that's a lame joke!"

Receiving no reply, he lit a joint and his tone became cool and sarcastic, "Y're nothin' but a lame-ass missionary."

"I won't let you lure Mark away from the shelter again!"

"He's eighteen, dude. Goes where he wants."

The object of their contention was pacing slowly in a circle, his expression flickering between vacancy, dread and irritation.

"The choice is between life and death, Mark," Sam shouted. "You don't want to OD like Tron! Or get rented to some john who'll slash your throat, like Raul!"

"Up y'r missionary sermon, shithead!" Reech, beating on a car chassis, soon had the stack under Sam trembling.

"Leave off, Reech, or the pile'll come down on you.

Colby couldn't actually see the speaker but the voice was female and the wolf-dogs were at her heels. Here was the old man's granddaughter.

"Did you call the police?" Sam called down. "I dropped my cell phone."

"Him I know," she said, pointing at Reech. "You're a trespasser."

Now Colby was able to see a blue flannel shirt, overalls and hiking shoes. One hand held a can of beer, the other a target pistol with a scope, making her the rat assassin. She wasn't a dyke, the junkman had told him, "Jus' too damn lazy t'make herself look pretty."

Colby also picked up flashes of her interest in Reech, especially when he asked:

"How's life treatin' yeh, Jewel?"

"What happened t'you fetchin' parts f'r Rasta's chopshop?"

"Changes, Jewel, a'ways changes."

The bloated sun was now melting into the jagged urban skyline, splattered in glass, steel and concrete reflections. Colby emerged in a shadow, sprang lightly to the van's roof, and settled cross-legged. He was entirely comfortable in a graveyard of dust, rust, old grease and rotting upholstery.

The only one to take note of his quick and nimble move was Mark. Who was then distracted by Reech lighting a joint and offering it. When Mark took it, Sam cried:

"That isn't what you need, Mark! You'll end up another drug zombie."

Jewel, studying Mark, asked, "Nothin' t'say, punk?" When Mark shrugged, she told Sam, "Some guys been out on streets s'long they can't change. An' if he eighteen…" She added a shrug of her own.

"He came back 'cause I'm th' good guy." When Reech took the joint from Mark, Colby perceived that Jewel hoped to be offered it. But she wasn't.

"You're a rotten pimp, Reech," Sam said. "You let johns abuse—"

"Hear that, kid? Sam wants yeh in his stable!" Reech, sneering and laughing, did a few flamenco steps. But stopped when he looked up and saw Colby perched on the van.

"So … now I know y'r secret squat."

He's making plans for me, Colby observed. *How interesting.*

"You stay away from him, Reech!" Sam cried. "He's a child."

"Wrong! He's a sly an' slippery runt, that's what."

"I'm a free range type."

Being small had not greatly troubled Colby until his peers hit their growth spurt and he was left behind. His "friends" teased and joked at first, but soon found him an embarrassment—especially when girls were around. But if his staying fifty-nine inches tall was vexation in middle school, it was an agony and a curse in high school. The hazing and harrowing never ceased.

All that had changed when he achieved Undeadness at nineteen. Now his being singled out by bullies was a source of entertainment. He wore gaudy and flashy colors and fashions calculated to bait. At that moment he was attired in plum satin trousers, a pink silk shirt with an embroidered collar, lilac velvet frock coat and patent leather half-boots with rhinestone buckles.

Jewel regarded him with a bent smile. "Yeah. Gramps said he was lettin' a freaky kid squat here. Gotta be you."

"Mark!" cried Sam, "don't let Reech touch that child!"

What Mark did was smile at Colby and say, "Hi. Call me No-name."

"Colby Todd, *ange d'mort.*" When he looked into No-name's clay-colored eyes, he saw a raw landscape of vulnerability and pain. Gangrene, he thought. So wounded he's septic.

"Don't play childish word games," Sam shouted at Colby. "Reech is an uberpervert and dope peddler!"

"Sam made Mark a bunch'a phony promises," Reech told Colby. "Lies an' cult trash."

"Ours is not a cult," Sam shouted back, "it's a shelter for abused and runaway kids."

Colby pointed at Sam. "She, not he." The wolf-dogs had read her scent and he'd found the truth floating in their minds.

Reech wheeled and grabbed No-name by the shirt. "No secrets, ain't that what yeh promised?" When he got no response, he slapped the hustler. The other cringed but made no other effort to avoid the blow.

Colby was consoled by his having always fought back.

"Stop brutalizing him!" Sam was tempted to climb down, but did not.

"This kid, he needs a master," Reech shot back, lighting another joint. "An' you ain't got the balls f'r it."

"Sam, why's he worth the trouble?" Jewel asked. "Lots'a street kids out there beggin' an' stealin', hustlin' an' dealin'."

"She likes tender stuff, angel cheeks," Reech told Colby. "Be on y'r bones next."

"Fallen angel," he corrected. *Killer angel.*

When Jewel offered Reech her can of beer, she was ignored.

Sam's eyes never left No-name, and now she said, "You should have stayed at the shelter. You had found the path to true salvation."

"He's *repented,*" Reech laughed. "Spit out y'r lies."

No-name transferred what little remained of the joint to a beaded roach clip and kept toking, his expression vacant, helpless.

Colby felt no urge to snuff Reech—yet. Let the events play out randomly, he thought, and hope to be surprised.

The pimp-dealer suddenly grabbed No-name and dragged him behind a wrecked, rusting bus—out of Sam's line of sight. He used large motions and added grunts, but Colby could see that he was pulling his punches. But No-name was so afraid of where the sham beating might lead that he begged and whimpered.

Sam, taken in by the ruse, cried, "If you're too gutless to use it, give me the gun!"

"He ain't said he wants help," Jewel answered.

"But let's get more light." She pressed a remote and lights atop the junkyard fence winked on.

Reech, growing impatient, put more muscle into his blows. When No-name writhed and sobbed, a frantic Sam started to climb down, overbalanced, and tore open her hand on a jagged metal edge. She fell the rest of the way with blood flowing darkly.

The sweet aroma of fresh blood now came to Colby from two directions, honing his appetite. But he was enjoying the show, and he'd learned to master his thirst.

Reech abandoned his ruse and ran toward Sam, who lay moaning on the ground. But Jewel forced him to stop with a shot that went by his ear and ricocheted off a door frame.

"No rapes in my yard, cowboy."

Reech was less concerned about her pistol than the wolf-dogs, which were staring hard at him and snarling, teeth bared and ears laid back.

Jewel now referred to Sam as "sister" and helped her up. Though dazed, Sam had the presence of mind to press her wound closed. With a final glance at No-name, she followed Jewel and the dogs to the wrecking yard office to receive first aid.

Two players exit. What next?

Colby was not surprised when Reech lit a joint and shifted his focus to him. "You eighteen yet?"

"A bit more than that—" Nineteen years alive plus thirty Undead.

"Run if yeh can..." whispered No-name, hugging himself against pain.

Colby noted Reech's every blink, twitch, and flex. The other was ready to pounce.

"Y'look 12 but're legal. Dude, y'could pull down big bucks doin' kiddie porn."

"I've heard this spiel before. I didn't just step off a Greyhound from Iowa."

Reech sucked his teeth. "Oh yeah. Mega bucks—*über bucks!*"

Colby remained motionless. No-name was rocking back and forth, his eyes closed.

"What's y'r story," the pimp-dealer toked and went on, holding the smoke in. "Runaway? Throw-away? Kill th' family?"

Colby could sense if not hear the gears, gimmals and escapements of the other's mind. He ignored No-name's silent anguish.

When Reech offered the joint, he said, "Not one of my vices."

"T'score big, y'gotta learn t'play dumb an' inno-cent."

"Calculate and connive but don't let it show, that what you mean?"

The other nodded. "Lot'a chicks got rich playin' that game."

Make your move, he thought. *Take the bait and dis-cover I'm also the trap.*

A moment more and Reech sprang forward, grabbed Colby's ankle, and jerked him from his perch. Only to have him wrench free, tumble away, and come to his feet smiling.

When the other dropped the half-smoked joint, No-name dove for it and also came up with a knife sheathed in Reech's boot.

"Talk 'bout a kid ridin' a death wish!" The pimp-dealer kicked at No-name, but the other eluded him, tossed the knife at Colby's feet, and curled up in a fetal position.

Reech pulled a switchblade from a hip pocket and flicked it open. "I'm gonna tag freaky graffiti on y'r sorry ass, punk."

But his attention shifted when the vampire broke the sheath knife in half and flipped it over his shoul-der. Reech then underwent a sea change when Colby closed with preternatural swiftness, took away the switchblade, then broke and discarded it.

"What party tricks can you offer?"

Reech stared with such fixity that he was nearly hypnotized before he awoke to the peril. Then a struggle of wills began.

"Afraid of losing control, aren't you?" Colby asked.

The other, resisting desperately, sweated freely but remained speechless.

"Let go. Drown in my will ... and be born again in my service."

When Colby finally exerted his full will, the oth-er's resistance shattered like matchwood.

"Is he really...?" asked No-name, awed but stay-ing on his knees.

"Helpless? Yes—feel free to punch or kick him." He took several joints from Reech's pocket and offered them to No-name, along with matches.

The hustler got up slowly, stiffly, grimacing with pain. "My real name is Les. Lester."

When he took the joints, Colby smiled and ex-tended his canine teeth. The other choked and nearly dropped the joint he'd just lit.

"Yo ... they ain't Halloween teeth..." said Les, vacillating between wonder and dread.

Colby sensed the wolf-dogs then heard ap-proaching footsteps. "Jewel and your would-be savior are returning. Best to put my new slave in the van for now."

"Let me hide too!"

"She's too horny for you?"

"Not her! She's all 'bout prayin' an' singin' hymns."

Les followed Reech into the van, if reluctantly. When both were inside, Colby sprang onto the roof. Where he was seated cross-legged when Sam arrived wearing a pair of paint-splattered work shoes. One hand was bandaged while the other held a flashlight.

"Where is Mark?" she demanded, searching with her light.

"With his savior."

She walked past swinging the beam from side to side. Meantime, Jewel and the wolf-dogs appeared. Along with her pistol she carried a bottle of beer.

"Both gone," he told Jewel, "back along the freeway to the underpass."

"Like I said," Jewel smirked. "Check b'fore yeh call 911."

"I can't believe he went with Reech!" Sam groaned then started to pray. But after a few seconds she asked Jewel for the pistol.

"Get real! I ain't lettin' you snuff nobody usin' my gun!"

"It's only to threaten him! Mark needs to be at the shelter."

"Then why'd he go with Reech?"

It only took a few seconds to decide Sam. "I'll find a way!" She hurried off toward the freeway. "Angels will show me the way!"

"Yo, y'got my shoes an' flash!" But Jewel soon gave up the chase. "I'd rather lose 'em than listen t'her noise."

She stopped to glance up at Colby, lit from behind by a rising gibbous moon. "I don't like you neither. I'm takin' back y'r welcome."

"I am the old man's guest, and this is his junkyard."

"I'll talk him 'round, you watch!"

"No. I think he likes me better."

She put down her beer, adjusted the sights on her pistol, and took aim.

Colby smiled. "Stick to rats. They're easy kills."

She let off a round that whistled past his ear. When he didn't even flinch, she threatened to sic the dogs on him.

"The wolf-dogs wish you smelled like yourself, the way the old man does. You offend them with your serial perfumes, from feet to hair."

Before she could take aim again, she found Colby in front of her and taking away the pistol. As she watched, he used an engine block to bend the barrel.

"You will now notice that the wolf-dogs like me better."

When she looked down and saw the pair glaring at her and baring their teeth, disbelief staggered her. Fear and confusion came next. She was under his spell before she knew it.

"Go home, drink some beers, and watch cable. Forget your dislike of me and the wolf-dogs will be their old selves."

As she and the dogs departed, a wide-eyed Les crept from the van.

"Awesome, man. Weird an' creepy ... but mos'ly awesome."

"How shall we dispose of Reech? Send him to play on the freeway? Watch big rigs and SUVs crush and grind him into road-kill pulp?"

Les shivered and giggled. "Video game ... only real."

"Yes. Stop thinking in game and voyeur terms. This will be real time crunch and splatter. Reech all mangled into juicy meat."

The other's expression quirked into a nervous smile then crumpled into worry lines. "Ah ... umm ... police, dude. Y'know, questions. An' I seriously hate questions."

Upon reflection, Colby agreed. His junkyard lair suited him. And as far as authorities were concerned, the old man was a die-hard Libertarian.

Les was blinking and biting his lip as he watched Reech emerge from the van at Colby's command. "But gotta do *somethin'*! Otherwise he'll make me worse'n dead."

Still on his master's string, Colby reflected, but eager to be liberated. Not so utterly gutted that only passive fatalism remains.

The other, now fever bright, whispered, "Is there a ... umm, a *squisher*?"

"A compactor? Two aisles over." He smiled. "An inspired choice. Wood-chippers are so noisy and untidy." *Who wants to see a machine vomit?*

A dazed Reech followed them docilely to the press. Between the moon and lights on the fence they could see a rusty pink Mustang waiting in the jaws.

"The scene is prepared for us," Colby said, cheerily.

A chill in the night air was not enough to keep Les from sweating. He even turned away while Reech stripped and clambered awkwardly through a window in a buckled door. But Colby suspected that Les' trembling was now mostly excitement and anticipation.

"He hates sissy colors … *totally hates!*" Les giggled, suddenly willing to watch.

"Reech may have been swaddled in blue after entering this life," he said, "but he is going out in pink—and other shades of red."

"Looks like somethin' in'a cage…"

"The honor of pushing the button belongs to you."

Les gaped at the green button, now paralyzed. Even when Reech, awaking to his peril, resisted Colby's influence and made a clumsy attempt to escape the Mustang.

"Why do you hesitate, Les? Suddenly miss his kind and affectionate ways? All those sweet and tender things he did to prove how much he loved and cherished you?"

Les' eyes hardened and his spine stiffened. Then a frenzy of hate welled up and he punched the "ON" button. And kicked Reech in the face, throwing him back from the window and his last hope of escape.

The compactor was alive and noisy now. Greased pistons and scarred steel walls were twisting, crumpling, cracking the pink chassis, bending and shearing and compressing. All to Reech's shrill keening farewell to life.

When its labors were done, the jaws opened and out tipped a cube of scrap as neat as a bundle of hide and bone vomited by an owl—except for its leaking blood.

Blood that Les washed away with urine. Then, less energized, he asked Colby, "Guess it must be my turn fr … fr whatever."

"The offering this rogue angel takes is a modest two ounces. Half a gill. I have a keen dislike of sloppy deranged gluttons."

Once inside the van, Les shed his clothes. Force of habit, Colby decided. He was glad as it exposed a heart inked above the other's heart. Biting into tattoos was a fetish of his.

The other lay back on the cushions and closed his eyes, his thin body relaxed and trusting. The blood Colby drew came spiced with marijuana and a trace of crack and meth. But the most pervasive flavors were greasy and sugary junk food. Favorites of his in his mortal years.

"Can I ask—umm, if you maybe you need a lookout? T'watch while y'sleep. And … and sometimes you could watch o'er me? I've been jumped a lot at night."

Why do I want or need a Renfield? he asked himself. He napped like a cat, never sleeping deeply. And rats would stand sentinel at his command.

He was done and was licking the tattoo clean when Les said, "Is it, ahh … umm, okay if I love you?"

Colby had viewed the turning of the Undead into romantic figures become a juvenile fad. But now that zombies had emerged as acceptable love objects, his revised posture was *Why not me?* He was more deserving of adoration than some rotting hulk.

A Menagerie of Tarot

Story by Melinda Moore
Illustration by Jag Lall

Cottonwood seeds dance across the twilight sky before snowing on the pierced and tattooed audience that waits on the lawn of the zoo. I look at the bark and my mind spins a story about a giant bear who scratched the first born cottonwood tree with her claws, scarring the tree and its offspring forever. Even though I just made it up, I could pass it off as an ancient Navajo legend to the Wiccan 101 crew that surrounds me. Lizzy would be so proud of her little pet then. I look at my long fingernails painted turquoise and wish I could change into a bear, but I'm stuck with the ability to change into a coyote, unless I want to return to the skinwalkers.

I roll over onto my stomach and watch my lover Lizzy telling skinwalker story number twenty-three to impress the young femmes—like she tried to impress me when we first met. She shifts her bottom on the grass, and I have a brief glimpse up her shorts. I should be turned on, but tonight her wrinkles and lack of muscle tone repulses me. Perhaps now that I'm older, I'm feeling too young for her. Or maybe it's because she won't shut-up about skinwalkers—ever.

A lobo howls in his section of the zoo, followed by his mate. The he lion answers and I start to sweat. Why haven't the Indigo Girls started yet? The stage over the duck pond is filled with instruments. I try to distract myself from Lizzy by watching the transvestite next to us make-out with two men. It looks awkward to me, but not as awkward as Lizzy moaning between the sentences of her story like she's about to orgasm. "And then the wolf hit the door before I had my window rolled up. His dull eyes started to glow as he changed into human form right before me." Her hands are above her head with her fingers splayed. The lamp light casts a halo behind her slim figure, and the young witches are entranced as I once was.

"If that had really happened, you'd be dead," I say. "He would've jumped right through your window and raped and eaten you, probably at the same time." I never talk about skinwalkers with Lizzy, not even to tell her that I was one, am one. I left, but it's one of those things you can't leave. She stares at me with grey eyes that match her silver hair. I love her hair. It's long and feels like mist in my hands. It's her only real magic.

She's been doing her shimmy and shake so long that she doesn't miss a beat. She laughs and says, "Of course Yanaha knows best, being from the rezzz and all." I hate the way she says rez. Why does she lengthen the z? A coyote howls right into my brain. I try to lay my head on my folded arms, but I have

Lizzy's attention now. "Why don't you do a reading for us, Yanaha?" I look up and my vision blurs like it always does when I begin to think about a reading. "You're in for a real treat now," she says as an aside to all the eager witches who don't care that I've called Lizzy on her sham. Young wiccans too desperately want to believe in magic.

In my mind, I see the cards in the order they will be drawn: the Three of Swords followed by the Eight of Swords. The reading will be for Lizzy. My vision clears and I say, "No."

She puts her hand on top of the head of a pretty blond and combs her fingers through the blond's hair. "Do one for Madison. Next week is the introduction to tarot, so now would be perfect to give them a tease."

I frown and say, "The cards are telling me the reading will be for you."

It's the first time her smile fades, but then it shines brighter than ever. "All the better." Madison sidles closer to Lizzy who wraps her arm around the girl: my replacement.

"Fuck you," I say and stand up.

Silence follows me as I weave through the crowd on the grass and wander the zoo path until I'm at the coyote exhibit. I look through the window surrounded by an adobe wall, but see my reflection instead of the two pathetic figures who are captured rather than wandering free in their native land. My black hair is braided and my chest is weighted down with a turquoise and silver necklace that matches my turquoise and silver belt. My skirt is ruffled down to my feet that are clad in leather sandals. Everything was bought for me by Lizzy, and received by me as someone receiving a blessing from a savior. Lizzy was my new beginning, where I could leave behind the evil and confusion of my childhood. But now I see I'm just something to dress up. She'll dress up Madison too—like a Barbie Doll.

I hear the crowd on the lawn murmuring because the show still hasn't started. Walking back on the path, I slip out of my shoes and drop my belt, followed by the clattering of my necklace. Once on the lawn I shed my blouse and skirt. I hear a few people shout, "Be free!" but I take no notice. The wicca class stares at my approach. I kneel down and dig the pack of tarot cards out of my purse. Once, Lizzy tried to give me a deck with Native American pictures. I threw it back at her and told her tarot cards were European and I could use the standard ones as well as everyone else. Why had I insisted on normal cards but let her dress me like an Indian doll sold at Old Town?

I toss my deck to her. "Shuffle them, but it doesn't matter. I know what the cards will be." I don't know where the power comes from. My first ten years were spent off the rez with a white family who sent me back after I predicted too many bike accidents and extramarital affairs. That's when the skinwalkers took an interest in me.

Lizzy stares at my mostly nude body, loving my brown skin and hating me for letting everyone else see it. She never wants to share me even though I'm supposed to turn a blind eye to her affairs with students. She shuffles the deck while still staring at me and then tries to hand it over.

I shake my head. "Deal for yourself. The first card will be the three of swords."

Lizzy begins to shuffle the cards again, thinking she will mess up whatever trick I have. She has never believed I have actual magic. I think she keeps me around hoping to discover my sleight of hand. She simpers at Madison to cut the deck. Madison divides it five times before putting them back together. Lizzy picks them up and draws the top card to her chest. Her eyes widen before she flicks it to the grass.

"The three swords in the heart represent the three women who fucked you over: your grandmother who cursed you for being a lesbian, your mother who wouldn't stand up for you and had her own lesbian affairs that she kept secret and your first lover who had the audacity to break up with you. The next card will be the eight of swords. Cross it over the first card."

The young witches exchange glances with each other before staring at Lizzy. She stares at me while she flips the top card over. The power of the moon is strengthening as the sky darkens and the woman on the card for the eight of swords blurs until she looks like me. "You love me and think you can keep me like a pet or a doll or freaking Rapunzel in the tower. The next card will be the Queen of Wands. Put it above these two."

Lizzy's hand shakes as she draws the Queen of Wands and places it above the first two. She loves it when I read for other people, but has never asked me to read for her. "You see yourself as the social mover, the one everyone adores, and they do adore you. Who could not? But the reality is you're the Queen of Swords." I pause and flip the top card over because I'm beginning to feel the pain Lizzy feels, but I can't stop the telling now. I place the Queen of Swords below the center cards. "You thrive on disaster. When your life is going great you make up stories about being attacked by skinwalkers, or you

have affairs when you know I love you. You want the fight because you're always like the Five of Cups."

I flip the card over and there is Lizzy on the card with her long silver hair hanging limp at the sides while she cries over the three spilled cups and ignores the two full cups behind her. "You're always thinking about your past, thinking about your loss. You're fifty-four now. Can't you move on so that you can face your future of the Moon."

Madison whips the deck away from me and shuffles over and over. By now the Indigo Girls are crooning on stage, but our little group is ignoring them as the rest of the audience is ignoring us. At least Lizzy has chosen someone who'll protect her. Maybe Madison has enough fire to stop the affairs in a way that I never could. She slams the deck back onto the grass and flips over the card. It's the Moon.

The dog and the wolf in the card begin to howl, calling to the animals around the zoo. Soon the cacophony of the animals is louder than the concert. "This card is your future. You don't know what it means but I do. And I won't tell you—not yet at least." My skin is itching. My legs feel like they're going to stand me up and run. My voice is deepening and I'm almost barking out the last cards. "Everyone thinks you have Strength, which you do but can never see it because you are too busy being paranoid like the man in the Nine of Wands which makes you The Fool."

On the word "fool" my bra hooks snap and my underwear rips. My muscles ripple as the hair on my skin grows longer. I pounce on Lizzy with all four paws. Her scent mixes with Madison's making me want to dine on them like the wolf in Little Red Riding Hood: first the crispy granny, then the lush girl. I bite my tongue.

Lizzy is crying now and tears from my eyes drip and roll down her cheeks. Don't turn over the last card. I think to her. It's The Tower. It'll only bring ruin. Burn the deck and let the ashes blow away. Free me from you and you'll free yourself.

I loosen my jaw and give Madison a lick, leaving a streak of slobber and blood on her cheek. I jump over the people next to us and run out of the zoo before the smell of so much meat in one place is too much for me to handle. The animals howl at me to free them, but I'll be going it alone for a long time.

An Empty House

The old house shakes,
No longer owned.
Winter winds threaten,
A home alone.

Floorboards creak,
Brittle boned.
A sudden draft,
Chimney moans.

Dust lays down
Like a virgin snow.
Shadows linger
They will not go.

Branch scratch on
Glass window panes.
Ceiling corners
Tattered webs claim.

The clench of quiet,
Suctions my lungs.
Breath is short,
An urge to run.

The grandfather clock
Is stuck at three.
For now, forever
Shall it be.

— Louise Webster

Adverts from _Tales of the Talisman_ Volume 161, Issue #2

afraid of life gaps?
we back up twice a second—
play nuclear tag
or try out sun spot surfing—
death's an option with CloneSure
hate human limits?
blend with another species—
bull-men go all night
shark-woman slash through boredom—
contact Chimera Inc now!
swamped by rising seas?
hold back the tide with DryDome—
make beachfront houses
ocean bottom habitats—
ask about free estimates

reality bitter?
sweeten it with Happy Chip—
swath slums with magic
see castles instead of tenements—
visit an implant tech soon

need more adventure?
be a cross-time explorer—
meet civilized spores
chat with talking dinosaurs—
call Pam's Portals for details

— Chuck Von Nordheim

Pool Sharks

Story by Dan Bracewell
Illustration by Paul Niemiec

Oliver stared at the sharks weaving in and out among the young women in the pool.

"Never mind them," Shaw said. He raised his can of Guinness over his immense belly and removed the Cuban cigar from his mouth. "They only nip at you every now and then—kind of like dogs."

Oliver counted the sharks, all near six feet in length. *Eight, nine ... ten ...*

Why were the women in the bikinis not afraid of them? They tossed a beach ball and laughed as if the sharks weren't even there.

Ravi Patel, a shy young man Oliver met at this week's business improvement conference, stood next to Oliver, twisting his ring around his finger over and over.

"He never said anything about sharks," Ravi said. "Never."

Ravi and Oliver met Augustus Shaw at the conference only a few nights ago. He was the headline speaker: "Overcome Your Fears."

Oliver always had problems being intimidated as long as he could remember: school bullies, sports, employers, confrontation, and beautiful women. His father used to call him a gutless wonder. After the conference, he and Ravi worked up the nerve to speak to Shaw about the matter in more depth. To their surprise, Shaw invited them to his mansion in Bel Air for the weekend for a private tutorial.

Shaw cracked open another beer. "Go on in. The water's fine and the women are finer."

Ravi shook his head and pushed his towel up into his arm pit. "No, thank you."

Oliver made no effort to get into the pool either. He sat on a lawn chair and watched the women throw the beach ball back and forth. They were the most gorgeous women he had ever seen. There was one in particular he thought was looking at him. She was a tall brunette with a sprinkle of freckles across her face. She beckoned him to join her. Oliver turned away. Even if there weren't sharks in the pool, he doubted he would have the courage to get in with her.

"Have you ever…," Ravi swallowed hard and ran his finger across the Hindu symbols on his ring. "Have you ever had one attack a swimmer?"

Shaw shook his head. "Nope. I have guests up here every few weeks. None of them ever get up the nerve to go in."

"Except the girls it seems," Oliver said.

Shaw blew smoke in Oliver's direction. Oliver didn't look at him. Shaw's eyes were like two deep holes and never seemed to blink.

"Go in," Shaw said again. "The girls are a lot of fun."

Oliver shook his head and looked away.

Shaw looked down at his cooler. "Well shit, out of beer. Why don't we go in the rec room and shoot some pool for a while? It's hot out here."

Oliver and Ravi followed Shaw through a glass door that overlooked the patio and into a large game room. Oliver froze when he saw the stuffed great white shark suspended by cables in the center of the room, its giant mouth filled with rows of sharp teeth gapping at him. Beyond it, above pool tables, video games consoles, dart boards, a bowling alley, and a large screen TV were shark's teeth, shark heads, and shark paintings.

Shaw went to the corner bar, opened a refrigerator, and pulled out a six pack. "You look like a White Russian type of guy, Oliver."

"Yes. How did you know?"

Shaw chuckled as he brought a bottle of vodka and Kahlua and a carton of cream to the counter. "I trust my instincts. It's one reason why I do so well in business."

Oliver walked under the great white. *God, how could a creature get so big?*

"You like him?" Shaw said as he mixed Ravi's drink, a concoction Oliver didn't recognize. "Just an inch short of nineteen feet. Caught him about six years ago a few miles off Long Island."

Shaw walked around the bar and handed Oliver and Ravi their drinks. Shaw took a cue stick and rack off the wall.

Oliver took a sip as Shaw racked up the balls. It was a little stronger than he liked. "How did you get this fascination with sharks?"

"They're great role models for a business man."

Ravi jumped at the cue ball's crack of the break. Three balls went in the pockets.

Shaw took the cigar out of his mouth. "Many would call me an eccentric man, but I know my business."

Oliver nodded. Shaw owned one of the largest commercial fishing companies in the U.S.

"And what I have to offer you boys," he said, "is the opportunity of a lifetime."

Shaw chalked his stick. The smoke from his cigar clouded his face as he peered at the young men. "One has to be tenacious and possess a killer instinct to succeed in business. That's why I like sharks. They're nature's perfect killing machines. That's what I want to be when I enter the business arena."

He sent a ball across the table into a corner pocket.

Oliver sighed. "I'm afraid I don't have the personality for it."

"Neither do I," Ravi said. He went behind Oliver, as if he were attempting to hide from Shaw.

"Bullshit. You know, I was once a lot like you two. It's why I invited you here. I look at you, and I see me ten years ago. Back then, I was in some two-bit restaurant company. They called me an executive partner, but I was just the boss's little gopher boy—get the coffee, fax this company, write this letter, call his wife. The son-of-a-bitch. I barely made 20k a year and no benefits for doing his lousy work."

The thirteen ball bounced twice off the sides and into a side pocket.

"I was hesitant, soft, broke, never been laid."

Oliver felt his cheeks flush and took a drink. Shaw was describing *him*.

"One has to confront his fears, boys." Another ball in the corner pocket. "It's the only way to succeed in life." He pointed at the great white. "Fear will eat you up just like this big bruiser if you don't."

Oliver's hand was shaking. He downed the rest of his drink. "Are you saying you are going to show us how to confront our fears?"

"I've already given you the opportunity to do so." Another ball cracked as it hit the pocket. "But you have refused. Despite the obvious rewards."

Shaw brought his cigar up to his face and gave a knowing grin. Oliver looked out the glass door and watched the beautiful girls play among the shadows of the sharks.

* * *

Oliver looked down at the silent pool from his upstairs window. The party ended hours ago. The women were gone. The moonlight reflected off the water. Occasionally, a fin broke the surface.

Shaw had given Oliver and Ravi a sumptuous dinner of swordfish and artichokes. Afterwards, Ravi confided to Oliver privately that he intended to leave first thing in the morning.

"That man scares me," Ravi said. "And I will never go into that pool of sharks, no matter what."

He wanted to know if Oliver would join him, but Oliver hadn't made up his mind on what he was going to do.

Shaw's words about rewards followed him the entire day. After their conversation in the rec room, Oliver had ventured more gazes at the beautiful women. He couldn't take his eyes off the brunette. She would twist one of her long locks around her finger and motion with her head, wanting him to come in with her. But then he would see the shadows lurking in the water. He couldn't do it.

Oliver wrapped his robe around, walked downstairs, and went out to the patio. He heard the swish of a tail in the water. At first he did not see anything, but then he saw a dark shadow patrolling the edge of the pool. He shivered and took a step away.

There seemed to be so many of them, much more than there had been during the day. Oliver could imagine himself stepping in the water and feeling jaws tearing into his thigh. Shaw said no one had ever been killed by any of the sharks. Maybe they were harmless. The women weren't afraid of them. The brunette didn't even seem to notice them. *God, she was so beautiful.*

Oliver walked to the stairs of the pool and looked down at the dark water. He took a deep breath and removed his robe. He placed a foot in the water, but a hand on his shoulder pulled him back.

It was Shaw. He brought his cigar to his mouth.

"Never swim at night."

Shaw walked to the pool edge. He was holding a five gallon bucket of bloody meat. He scooped it up in his hand and tossed a bit in at a time. The pool foamed with the sharks' thrashing.

"Gorgeous aren't they?"

Oliver hugged himself. "Terrifying is more like it."

"I knew there was something about you, Oliver," Shaw said. "You're different than all the others I've brought up here. In the morning, show the same type of courage you showed tonight. If you do, by this time tomorrow you will be a new man. Now go get some sleep."

When Oliver walked back inside the house, he happened to take a look back. Strange. For a moment it looked as though Shaw were eating from the bucket.

* * *

Oliver walked into Shaw's study in the morning. Shaw was sitting at a big desk talking on the phone. He chomped his cigar.

"You tell that son-of-a-bitch I said to sell those boats. I don't care what he has to say about it. You tell him to do what I say or I'll come down there personally and kick his ass."

He slammed the receiver down and gave Oliver a big grin.

"Nothing like business."

He clapped his hands and stood from the desk. He was wearing polka-dot swim trunks. His hairy chest was sunburned from the day before.

"You ready to swim?"

Oliver nodded. He followed Shaw toward the patio.

"Ravi's gone," Oliver said. He had just checked his room. The young man must have been scared out of his wits. He hadn't even bothered to say goodbye.

"Yep," Shaw said. "Ravi was just like the rest of them: chicken shit. Happens all the time."

The patio was alive with the sounds of laughing women. Two beach balls were zipping back and forth across the pool. A busty blond turned on a radio, ran across the lawn, and jumped in.

The tall brunette with the freckles was again at the deep end of the pool. When she saw Oliver, she gave an inviting grin.

Shaw put his cigar out in a stone ash tray and rubbed his hands together. "Nothing like a morning swim with a pool full of beauties."

He did a cannonball right in the middle of the pool. The girls laughed and swam out to join him. Shaw surfaced laughing.

"Come on in, Oliver."

Oliver walked to the edge, but had difficulty seeing the women for the black shapes circling Shaw. Yet the man was unafraid. The brunette caught Oliver's eye. She smiled.

He put his hand on his heart, hoping to slow its beating, and stepped into the pool. The women and Shaw cheered as he waded out waist deep. A shark came near him. He froze. It swam right by. A woman took his arm and led him out deeper.

"Ha!" Shaw smacked the water as three women flocked around him on the side of the pool. "You see? There is nothing to fear, but fear itself. You're the first, Oliver. By damn, you are the first!"

The sharks swam past Oliver as if he wasn't even in the pool. Once or twice their fins or rough skin brushed against him, but there never was any harm.

A hand touched his. When he looked up, the brunette was there. Water dripped down her wet hair, down her cheeks, and to her neck. Her eyes were black as a raven's wing. She pulled him to her and wrapped her arms around his chest. He felt dizzy as she kissed his throat and ears.

"What did I tell you, Oliver?" Shaw said. "Are the rewards not worth it?"

Oliver did not see the sharks anymore.

* * *

Oliver sat down at Shaw's desk. He punched in numbers on his telephone. He was angry and ready for a fight. The phone on the line rang. A moment later, a voice answered.

"Richey? Is that you? Yeah? Well, this is Mike Oliver. Did you send out the company portfolios like I told you?"

There was stammering on the other side.

"I thought so. You're fired Richey. I don't want to see any of your…" Oliver hesitated.

"Go ahead," Shaw said as he racked up a game of pool. "Cuss, goddamn it."

"Any of your *fucking shit* when I get back on Wednesday. You hear me?"

"There ya go," Shaw chuckled.

Oliver closed his phone and tossed it to the side.

"Nothing like business," Shaw said. "See? Fear is no longer an obstacle."

Oliver chose a cue stick from the wall, sighted up the cue ball, and broke. A ball went into the corner pockets.

"God, I could laugh in the face of the devil and not be afraid." Oliver walked around the table to make another shot. "How did you come across such a cure for fear?"

Shaw blew smoke rings across the great white's belly.

"Remember that little shit job I had about ten years ago?"

"Yeah."

"Well, the company had a conference in the Dominican Republic one year. By about the second day, I had enough of that asshole employer of mine. I rented a small boat and went out to one of them little islands off the coast. Bad day to go out—a storm was coming and I got blown way out to sea. By the time the storm passed, I was out in the middle of nowhere, with no gas. I could see an island not too far away, but I was drifting away from it. I was about to swim for it when I noticed the water was full of sharks."

"Hard spot."

"Yeah. But, I was going to die either way so decided to swim."

He pointed out a scar on his side. "I had gotten all the way to shore before I was nipped."

Shaw walked around the pool table and glanced at the women outside. "The local natives helped me get back to the main land. When I saw that son-of-a-bitch employer of mine, I told him he could go to hell."

He stuck his cigar in his mouth and flashed his toothy smile.

"The rest is history."

* * *

Oliver returned to the pool and swam with the

women. The brunette was all over him. Within half an hour he wanted more than just her tongue in his mouth and her hands in his swimsuit.

"Why don't we go upstairs to my room?" he said.

He never said that to a woman before.

She traced his face with her finger and smiled. Shaw chuckled as they left the patio.

She was as fierce as a barracuda and afterwards they lay on the bed, their limbs intertwined. Oliver watched the sky darken through the window and soon the sounds of the party diminished. The brunette picked up her swim suit and stood to leave. Oliver grabbed her hand.

"Why not stay here tonight?"

She reached down and kissed him. Her lips were so luscious. When he pulled her bottom lip to taste her once more, he froze. Her teeth were triangular with serrated edges. Oliver released her. She gave him a thin smile and walked out the door.

Oliver scrambled out of the bed and rushed to the window. It was almost dark. All the women were gone, but there were now over a dozen sharks in the water. Oliver saw the brunette run across the patio and dive into the deep end. She looked in his direction before she changed from a lithe beautiful woman to a six foot shark on contact.

Oliver felt the color drain from his face. *It's a trick. A god damn trick!*

His eyes fixed on the long shadow now mingling among the others. In his mind, the image of her serrated teeth flashed.

"Shaw!"

Oliver stormed down stairs, not bothering to grab his clothing. Oliver found Shaw in the kitchen chopping meat in the sink with a cleaver. Oliver became acutely aware of the smell of blood.

Shaw turned and looked at him with bored eyes.

"Yeah, Oliver, what is it?"

"You know fucking well what it is!" Oliver pointed at the patio.

"What? Her? What does it look like she is?"

"I have no fucking clue!"

Shaw tossed a chunk of flesh into a bucket and shrugged. "I don't know what they are either. When I was on that island all those years ago, they were the only inhabitants. I freaked out, like you, when I saw them turn into sharks at night. But during the day, they were so fucking gorgeous. I finally decided that the rewards were worth taking a risk, just like you did. Not only did I get the women, I also lost my fear. And there is more Oliver—strength, prowess, virility—all

from swimming with those women."

Shaw gave him a grin. His teeth were shark-like. Oliver touched his own. Sharp. Serrated.

Oliver recoiled. "What—what have you done to me?"

"Relax. You won't turn into a shark. We aren't the same as them."

Oliver touched his teeth again. "You piece of shit! You lied to me!"

"I didn't lie to you. I told you you would lose your fear if you swam with the sharks and you did. You're just pissed because you just got laid by a fish."

Oliver seized Shaw's collar. Shaw yanked it free.

"Quit being such a dumb ass," Shaw snapped. "You were a scared shitless little fuck when I brought you here but I made a man out of you. And now all you can do is bitch."

Shaw hacked into the meat with his cleaver and tossed it into one of the buckets on the floor. As he grabbed another hunk, Oliver froze. Shaw had grabbed a human hand. A silver ring with Hindu symbols was around one of the fingers.

Oliver's hand went to his mouth. "Oh, God…"

Shaw looked at him quizzically then saw him staring at the ring. He plucked it from the finger, studied it for a moment, and tossed it on the counter. It rolled off the side and onto the floor with a ping.

Oliver felt dizzy. He collapsed against the wall. Tears rolled down his cheeks.

What have I done?

"No big deal," Shaw said. "Ravi was a pussy. No one will miss him. There will be others who will come and won't cut it, which works out for us and the sharks. We need a little human protein in our diet every now and then. It's something you'll get used to pretty quick. Tastes like pork."

Shaw walked out of the kitchen and onto the patio. Through the window Oliver watched him toss the chum into the pool. Every few throws he would bring the mess up to his mouth and take a bite.

Oliver's knees buckled and he fell to the floor. His eyes wandered to the nearest bucket. He wanted to taste it too. His teeth scraped against each other at the smell. He dug his hands into the bloody mess and brought it to his mouth as he sobbed. It tasted so good.

As he reached in for another mouthful, his eyes fell upon the silver ring lying on the floor, dark and bloody.

No.

His breathing increased as a rage built inside him. *No!*

Oliver hurled the bucket across the floor and stalked out onto the patio. Shaw looked up at him, blood smeared around his mouth.

"I don't want to hear any more of your shit tonight, Oliver. Sleep on it and we will talk tomorrow when you feel better."

"I don't think we have completely lost our fear," Oliver said.

Shaw brought his cigar up to his mouth. "Oh? What makes you say that?"

Oliver looked at the pool and back at Shaw. Shaw's eyes widened.

"Oliver, no, not at night—"

Shaw flung up his hands as Oliver leaped across the patio and tackled him into the pool. Through the foam and tangle of fins, Oliver watched a large shape bite into his thigh. Soon he and Shaw's blood filled the water and once again they both knew fear.

Hero. Small stature.
Calm essence. Balanced at
the edge of two worlds.
Bitter winds wrap in land
of moss and rain.
Moist.
Damp.
Distant richness.
Dim land of promise.
Path to the fertile.

The Epic of Weeden by Jerry Shippee

Jutting ironstone of living destruction. Blocked. These creatures astride the gates of Albion. Magogoli giants challage all passage. Rise yon monsters.
Rise to do battle!

Slash. Crush. Cleave.
Mighty blows struck. Ground sways. Power held for ages
strikes! Fury. Wrath. Ire. Blades find the mark. Mortal
wounds fell the
craggy mass

Battle lost. Children of Gog vanquished.
Over precipiece fall to murk of sea.
Torment the land no more.
Victor holds the spoils.
Weeden.
Small.
Mighty.
Victorious!

This summer, get away from it all with *Tales of the Talisman!*

What if you could slip back in time and become the person who wrote every hit song you know and love today? Wayne Faust introduces us to a man who does just that.

Slow, shambling zombies are a thing of the past. Steven J. Blitz follows a man trapped in an apocalyptic wasteland who must run for his life from a very agile zombie.

Douglas Empringham is back with a new tale of Rhing and Folie. This time, they meet a woman who flies a steam-powered ornithopter.

Jack Herbert asks what happens when love toys become sentient and learns that other emotions can come into play.

Escape with these and other stories this summer in *Tales of the Talisman!*

Don't miss a single issue, subscribe to *Tales of the Talisman*
at www.talesofthetalisman.com today!

One year $24.00 (That's 25% off the cover price)

While you're there, check out the other great books and
audio available from Hadrosaur Productions

Subscriptions also available by mail at:

Hadrosaur Productions, P.O. Box 2194, Mesilla Park, NM 88047-2194

About the Contributors

Dan Bracewell lives in the oldest city in the United States with his wife, two daughters, and an overweight cat. Over the years, he has been a drummer, missionary, archaeologist, exchange student, museum curator, video game developer, and ghost tour guide. Currently, he is broke, barely employed, but has never been happier. Like every other aspiring writer, he spends what little time he has working on the good ol' American novel. "Pool Sharks" is his first sale and he couldn't be more thrilled.

Ian Brazee-Cannon is a writer, film maker, game designer, podcaster as well as a husband and father. His short stories have been published in *The Fifth Di...*, *Wondrous Web Worlds*, *Forgotten Worlds*, *Tales of the Talisman* and May-December Publications' anthology *Say Goodnight to the Bad Guy*. A collection of his works titled *My Delusions of Godhood* can be found at Amazon.com. Ian has been working with Nomadic Delirium Press on supplements for the Ephemeris RPG. He is one of the founders and regular co-hosts on the Amateur Skeptics podcast and has been a guest on other skeptic podcasts. Ian is also involved with Dangling Carrot Films, Running Riot Productions and Ijin Productions as a writer and director on their projects.

M.E. Brines spent the Cold War assembling atomic artillery shells and preparing to unleash the Apocalypse (and has a medal to prove it). But when peace broke out, he turned his fevered, paranoid imagination to other pursuits. He spends his spare time scribbling another steampunk romance occult adventure novel, which despite certain rumors absolutely DOES NOT involve time-traveling Nazi vampires!

A member of the British Society for Psychical Research, he is a long-time student of the occult, a committed Christian, and author of three dozen books, e-books, chapbooks and pamphlets on esoteric subjects such as Alien Abduction, Alien Hybrids, UFOs, Conspiracies, Mind Control the Falun Gong, esoteric Nazism, the Knights Templar, astrology, magick, the Bible, the spear of Longinius and Christian discipleship. His work has also appeared in *Challenge* magazine, *Weird Tales*, *The Traveller Chronicle*, *Midnight Times*, *The outer Darkness*, *Empirical* and *The Willows* magazine.

Beth Cato's poetry can be found in *The Christian Science Monitor*, *The Pedestal Magazine*, *Every Day Poets*, and on various pieces of paper crammed into her purse. She lives in Arizona, but is from Hanford, California. Her website is http://www.bethcato.com.

Robert Collins has had three SF novels published: *Monitor*, *Lisa's Way*, and *Expert Assistance*. He's had two fantasy novels published, *Cassia* and *The Opposite of Absolute*, as well as several short story collections. He has also had a coming of age novel published called *True Friends*. Robert has had stories and articles appear in periodicals such as *Marion Zimmer Bradley's Fantasy Magazine*, *Tales of the Talisman*, *Space Westerns*, *Sorcerous Signals*, *Wild West*, and *Model Railroader*. He's had two biographies and several other nonfiction books about Kansas history published.

Andrew Conde writes constantly and sends it all to Kelley. Sometimes she likes it. Contact him: Andrew Conde 24051, WMCI, 7076 Road 55F, Torrington, Wyoming 82240.

Jennifer Crow's fiction has appeared in a number of venues, including DAW Books' *Ages of Wonder* anthology and Elektrik Milk Bath Press's anthology of ocean fantasies. She lives near a waterfall in western New York State, and is currently working on a novel involving Russian necromancers and revolutionaries.

Douglas Empringham has had fiction accepted by *Black Gate*, *Space and Time*, *The Lamp-Post*, *Leading Edge*, *The Armchair Aesthete*, *Rosebud* and other genre and literary magazines including both *Tales of the Talisman* and *Hadrosaur Tales*.

As a child, **Kathy Ferrell** refused to share her crayons, preferring to eat them all herself. Today she is an artist and writer working from her decidedly sinister 19th century home, nestled deep in the backwoods of Appalachia. When not creating, she can be found wrapped in a shawl, drinking tea and wondering what on earth could be making that incessant creaking on the stair. She also uses the internet, in spite of being warned.

Paintings: cuposwank.carbonmade.com
Words: cuposwank.wordpress.com

Neil T. Foster is a freelance artist who lives in Australia. He has penciled and inked various comic books, recently completing an online comic—*Beware the*

Beast—for the official International *Planet of the Apes* Fan Club. He has done illustrations and painted covers for various SF fanzines, CD booklets and computer games. His work includes everything from illustration, cartoons, logos and comic strips to artwork for action figure packaging. His illustrations and painting have also appeared in *The Corpse* and *Black Petals* Magazines.

Laura Givens is a Denver Based author and artist. Her art has graced the covers of numerous publishers' books and magazines. She has provided illustrations for *Orson Scott Card's Intergalactic Medicine Show, Jim Baen's Universe, Talebones, Science Fiction Trails* and *Tales of the Talisman*. Her work may be viewed at www.lauragivens-artist.com. In 2010 she naively decided she could probably write stories as good as many she had illustrated. She has sold works ranging from zombie stories to space operas. She was co-editor and contributor to *Six-Guns Straight From Hell*, a weird western anthology, and is art director for *Tales of the Talisman* magazine.

Ken Goldman, an affiliate member of the Horror Writers Association, is a former Philadelphia teacher of English and Film Studies. He has homes on the Main Line in Pennsylvania and at the Jersey shore depending upon his mood and his need for a tan. His stories have appeared in over 670 independent press publications in the U.S., Canada, the UK, and Australia. Since 1993 Ken's tales have received seven honorable mentions in The Year's Best Fantasy & Horror. He has written three books: his book of short stories, *You Had Me at Arrgh!! : Five Uneasy Pieces* (Sam's Dot Publishers); a novella, *Desiree,* (Damnation books); and *Donny Doesn't Live Here Anymore*, a book of five short stories (A/A Productions). Ken would be famous except for the fact nobody seems to know who he is. He looks forward to the day when he and Stephen King are called to the dais and someone asks "Who is that guy standing next to Ken Goldman?"

Morland Gonsoulin is a traditionally trained artist and avid science fiction fan living in Colorado Springs, Colorado. He has done artwork for various publications before, including *Tales of the Talisman* Magazine.

K.S. Hardy has had his poetry in *Talebones, Weird Tales, Mythic Delirium, Dreams and Nightmares,* and many others. His short stories have appeared in *Tales of the Talisman, Beyond Centauri,* and *Lore* where Brian

Lumely took notice, and others now more obscure. He has received numerous honorable mentions in the *Best Fantasy and Horror* anthologies and was nominated for the Rhysling Award.

Stace Johnson spent the first five years of his life in Hatch, NM, before moving to Colorado with his parents in 1970. He now lives near Denver with his wife and pets, and works in the IT field. His poetry has been featured on the Apex Magazine website (http://www.apexbookcompany.com/2013/02/what-makes-you-die-poem-winner/) and the now defunct RomanticShortLoveStories.com. He received Honorable Mention in the Fall 2009 Writers of the Future contest, and he has written over thirty non-fiction articles for computer magazines. He is a fan of the poetry of Gerard Manley Hopkins, the inspiration for the pastiche in this issue, and intends no disrespect to Hopkins or his memory.

Tom Kelly received a degree in Graphic Design from Lycoming College and holds a master's degree in Sequential Art from the Savannah College of Art and Design. Tom has worked for several years producing graphic design and illustration for numerous design and production companies. As a freelance artist, Tom has produced illustrations and cartoons using a wide variety of classical and electronic techniques. Tom focuses on creating dynamic visuals by fusing together a wide variety of elements into one thought-provoking illustration. Tom's sequential work focuses on the power of bold black and white elements as well as the power of graphic design to relate a narrative.

C.J. Killmer was born and raised in the Sunshine State, where he spent his childhood fishing for sharks and searching the Everglades for the Skunk Ape, Florida's answer to Sasquatch. He spends his days teaching history at a college in North Florida, but when the sun goes down he writes horror, sci-fi, and crime stories. His short fiction has appeared in *Science Fiction Trails, Ray Gun Revival*, and the anthologies *Dead Bait* and *Space Cops*. Check out his website, cjkillmer.com, or drop him a line at chris@cjkillmer.com.

David C. Kopaska-Merkel describes rocks (and the holes in them) for the State of Alabama. He lives with an artist and some furry children in an urban farmhouse with a yellow "tin" roof. He collects wormholes & the like. He was born in Virginia, but has lived in the home of the crookneck as long as anywhere. Kopaska-Merkel has published in the neighborhood of a thousand poems, short stories, reviews, and essays over the past quarter century. He won the Rhysling award of the Science Fiction Poetry Association for best long poem in 2006 for a collaboration with Kendall Evans. Kopaska-Merkel has edited and published *Dreams and Nightmares* magazine since 1986, and has published a few Rhysling winners over the years.

DN website:

http://dreasandnightmares.interstellardustmites.com

Flash fiction at: www.dailycabal.com.

Blog, featuring a daily poem, at:

http://dreamsandnightmaresmagazine.blogspot.com

@DavidKM on twitter.

Jag Lall works in both the comic book industry and book illustration field producing bold, atmospheric artwork. The former is his lifeblood and he is currently working on a project to raise awareness of different cultures.

William Landis Jr. is a graduate student from North Carolina who is currently considering other ways to procrastinate.

Jim Lee, a lifelong resident of Windber, Pennsylvania and frequent contributor to *Tales of the Talisman* is Associate Editor for Market News with The Penn Writer, a newsletter for writers in his state. Other recent sales can be found in *The Bracelet Charm, Hustler Fantasies* and several titles from Sam's Dot Publishing.

Faith, nature, molecular biology (a former researcher) and membership in the SFPA help to inspire **Lauren McBride's** stories and poems, which have appeared in various science fiction, fantasy, horror, nature and children's publications including *Tales of the Talisman, Scifaikuest* (featured poet, August 2010) and *The Drabbler* (second place, issue 21). She shares a love of laughter, science and the ocean with her husband and two children.

Erika McGinnis has been painting and drawing since she was very young. She earned her Bachelor of Fine Arts from Boise State University (go Broncos!) in 1998 with an emphasis in art history. Erika is a member of the International Association of Astronomical Artists (www.IAAA.org) and is an avid science fiction reader, from where a lot of her inspiration comes. Her art has shown at various scifi conventions around the country and has won "Best of Show" quite a few times. Erika instructs watercolor classes for the Idaho Academy of fine Arts and youth art through Young Rembrandts. She has done numerous illustrations for books, CD covers and magazines, such as *Farscape - Season Three, With Friends Like These*, and *Tales of the Talisman*. Her **New Star Tarot Deck** and **Boxed Set** are available through Barnes and Noble and various online booksellers.

Erika owns a company called *Under the Cobalt Sky, Llc.*, which carries a line of products featuring her artwork for yoga wear with proceeds benefiting the Humane Society and jewelry that emphasizes the different ages of art history. These are available at museum shops and online on her website: www.erikamcginnis.com.

Erika lives in Boise, ID, with her husband, jazz saxophonist Sandon Mayhew and their dog, Thelonious.

F.T. McKinstry is the author of the fantasy series *The Chronicles of Ealiron*, a short story collection *Wizards, Woods and Gods: Tales of Integration*, and *Water Dark*. She has published stories and art in *Tales of the Talisman* and *Aoife's Kiss*. She lives in northern New England with a loving and inspirational raft of books, cats, fishes and gardens. Find out more at ftmckinstry.com.

Melinda Moore lives in Albuquerque, NM: The Land of Enchantment. Possessing a love of adventure, she has been a dancer, professional musician, music educator, recipe creator, parent and now published author. She gives away designer coffee on her blog as well as running a monthly writing contest based on photographs. Check out her current thoughts and all the goodies at www.enchantedspark.com.

Lance J. Mushung graduated from the Georgia Institute of Technology with an aerospace engineering degree. He worked for over 30 years with NASA contractors in Houston, Texas performing engineering work on the Space Shuttle and its payloads. Now retired, he writes science fiction.

Paul Niemiec plays guitar in a swing band—atomic pablo. Check it out at myspace.com. Paul's first job in high school was an art job doing safety filmstrips for hard-rock miners. After that, the office situation—smooth jazz radio, and chain-smoking co-workers—really put him off commercial art.

After a long hiatus, he got back into drawing. Paul

was trying to figure out which way a camel's front legs bent, and he decided to go to the zoo to draw camels. Later, he met some of the Squid Works guys at a figure drawing class.

Terrie Leigh Relf, a lifetime member of the Science Fiction Poetry Association and an active member of the Horror Writers Association, graduated from Bennett/Stellar University's Neuro-Linguistic & Hypnotherapy® Life-Trance-Formation Coach Program, and now specializes in working with writers and other creative individuals.

Formerly of Sam's Dot Publishing and Alban Lake Publishing, Relf will continue to host the Drabble Harvest contest publication.

Recent releases include *Letting Out the Demons and Other Poems*, illustrated by Marge Simon, (available at **http://elektrikmilkbathpress.com/bookstore**), and *The InterGalactic Cookbook*, co-authored with, and illustrated by, Marge Simon and Sandy DeLuca (available at **http://store.albanlake.com/product/ intergalactic-cookbook-the/**). Her poetry collection, *An Untoward Bliss of Moons*, is upcoming from Alban Lake in 2014.

You may contact her at tlrelf@gmail.com. Her website, terrieleighrelf.com is currently under construction.

James Frederick William Rowe is a young and up and coming author and poet out of Brooklyn, New York, with works appearing in *Heroic Fantasy Quarterly*, *Big Pulp*, and *Andromeda Spaceways Inflight Magazine*. When not writing fantasy, science fiction, and horror fiction and poetry, he is pursuing a Ph.D. in philosophy and works in a variety of freelance positions.

"Star Song of the Granger" is the first work of his to appear in *Tales of the Talisman*, and is dedicated to the memory of his grandmother, Elizabeth Sundberg (1918-2011).

The poet's website can be found at: http://jamesfwrowe.wordpress.com

Jeff Samson's previous work has appeared in *Nature* Magazine, *Daily Science Fiction*, *Lore*, *Jabberwocky*, *Perihelion*, *Every Day Fiction*, and *Brain Harvest*.

With over a million words in print **Patrick Thomas** keeps busy writing the fantasy humor series *Murphy's Lore* (*Tales From Bulfinche's Pub*, *Fools' Day*, *Through the Drinking Glass*, *Shadow of the Wolf*, *Redemption Road*, *Bartender of the Gods*, *Nightcaps* and *Empty Graves*)

as well as the *After Hours* spin offs *Fairy With A Gun*, *Fairy Rides the Lightning*, *Dead To Rites*, *Rites of Passage*, and *Lore & Dysorder*. His Mystic Investigators paranormal mystery series has grown to include *Bullets & Brimstone* and *From The Shadows*— both with John L. French; and *Once More Upon A Time* and the upcoming *Partners In Crime*—both with Diane Raetz. He co-edited *New Blood* and *Hear Them Roar*. Patrick's syndicated humorous advice column Dear Cthulhu has been collected in *Have A Dark Day*, *Good Advice For Bad People*, and *Cthulhu Knows Best*. A number of his books are part of the set and props department at the CSI television show and have been spotted on the show. His urban fantasy *Fairy With A Gun* has been optioned by Laurence Fishburne's Cinema Gypsy Productions for film and TV. Drop by www.patthomas.net to learn more or find out about The Patrick Thomas Show mockumentary.

Originating from the UK but now residing in the Canary Islands, **Teresa Tunaley** finds more time to devote to her love of art and writing. For more than 30 years she has been doodling traditionally with pencils and dabbling with watercolors.

Along with published stories and poetry, she can be credited with award winning cover art and illustrations for author stories. Her work can be seen online and in print across the UK, US, Canada and Europe.

"I like to think that I am very versatile in my choice of subject matter—my new surroundings provide the inspiration for me to paint on a daily basis and the fact that others may enjoy my work gives me the confidence to continue."

Louise Webster graduated Magna Cum Laude with a degree in Communication Arts. Immediately after college, she wrote the evening news for a small cable TV company.

Staying home to raise her children afforded her the opportunity to write poetry for many of the small presses. She has also written an article for a psychology book, a horticulture magazine and won a contest on the history of Lake Ronkonkoma.

Louise has had poetry accepted by June Cotner for two of her anthologies, *Dog Blessings* and *House Blessings*. She had a short story published in *Nurturing Paws* edited by Lynn C. Johnston.

Most recently, her poetry has been accepted by *Tales of the Talisman*, edited by David Lee Summers.

Neil Weston resides in the UK. His speculative

poems can be found lining such journals, books and magazines as *Eye to the Telescope, Mobius: a journal for social change, Scifaikuest, Hungur Magazine, Futuredaze* (an anthology of YA science fiction), *Space and Time* Magazine and an earlier edition of *Tales of the Talisman*. He also has several flash fiction pieces adorning cyberspace.